# Mary Watson

# And

# The Departed Doctor

Fred Thursfield

Paperback ISBN  978-1-78092-918-7
ePub ISBN  978-1-78092-919-4
PDF ISBN  978-1-78092-920-0

Published in the UK by MX Publishing
335 Princess Park Manor, Royal Drive, London, N11 3GX
www.mxpublishing.com
Cover design by www.staunch.com

## Prologue –2015

The 1922 discovery in the Valley of the Kings by Howard Carter and George Herbert, 5th Earl of Carnarvon of Tutankhamen's nearly intact tomb received worldwide press coverage. It sparked a renewed public interest in ancient Egypt, for which Tutankhamen's burial mask, now displayed in the Cairo Museum, remains the popular symbol.

---

There was more than a little reason to believe that King Tutankhamen may have been murdered. The two principal suspects, Aye who succeeded him as king, and General Horemhab who in turn succeeded Aye to the throne, both appear to have been powerful men who, in effect, ruled Egypt while King Tutankhamen, was a child.

It would not be unreasonable at all to believe that, as the King grew into a young man, the two elder men would have resented losing much of their power. Furthermore, at the time of his death, King Tutankhamen, was certainly old enough to have sired an heir to the throne himself, which would have at least technically eliminated Aye and Horemhab from ever ascending the throne.

It is also noteworthy that the young King was greatly loved in ancient Egypt for restoring the Amun priesthood after the death of his presumed heretic father, Akhenaten. However, this was almost certainly the work of Aye and General Horemhab, who could have even resented Tutankhamen receiving all the glory of their work.

Finally, there was the matter of the Kings widow, Ankhespaton, who was apparently forced to marry Aye after King Tutankhamen's death. Only a short time later, she disappeared from the annals of history, leading to speculation that she too might have been murdered.

These circumstances all contribute to an ancient mystery, and much intrigue, a situation that was not completely uncommon in the Egyptian royal court. Attempts had, and would be made to murder pharaohs, a few of which were successful. Usually, these seem to have been plots with the purpose of eliminating one person to further the ambitions of another or of others

Mary Watson

And

The Departed Doctor


As related from the case notes of Mary N. Morstan

London, 1923

# Chapter 1

The last day of my overseas holiday in New York City in 1922 was spent in the company of my cousin Mrs. Alice Eastman and my overseas travelling companion Mr. Sherlock Holmes. Together that evening we three had attended a performance by Harry Houdini (a world famous American magician and escape artist) at the Hippodrome Theatre.

After the show had ended, but just before leaving to return to Alice's home I had unexpectedly found myself quickly making my way through the theatre and back stage to discover the reason for Sherlock's sudden and mysterious failure to reappear from one of the magic tricks.

Not finding an immediate answer to my dilemma for a moment I was at a loss...then receiving a note from Mr. Houdini (explaining the reason for Sherlock's disappearance) I found myself just standing there not knowing what to do next.

After a time realizing that I could not undo what had just taken place (or for that matter bring the detective back) I heard myself saying (in rather a quiet voice) certainly an unplanned, unexpected, and somewhat wistful and absent good bye to Sherlock

The next morning after consoling Alice (about the recent circumstances concerning her husband) then saying fare well to her...I alone, without the company of the consulting detective boarded the RMS Majestic (an ocean liner of the White Star line) for my return voyage to Southampton from there by train onto London.

After a short time my life at home (with all it was) soon returned to its customary course and pace and I found myself once again settling back into the quiet, and predictable daily domestic routines I had grown accustomed to in the last three years.

But as 1922 became 1923 I was becoming more aware that with having assisted Sherlock in successfully solving two recent cases (one previously in England and now one in America) certain personal characteristics about myself had begun to change.

Most noticeably now when chronicling or writing instead of always closing with my married last name 'Watson' I found myself occasionally signing a completed document or personal letter with my maiden surname 'Morstan.'

Because of this encouraging transformation I was becoming more assured and confident of my place in the world. I no longer felt that I must continue to live in the shadow of my late husband's fame and could now at last be my own person.

I had also come to realize through Sherlock's unexpected acknowledgement of my valued assistance and contributions to his cases during dinner one evening (at the Houdini's) that in my own right if called upon for any reason I would eagerly take up the role of a capable solo detective.

As the inevitable outcome of my acquired and now well tested abilities of deduction, reasoning and in at least in one instance disguise (in New York City) I had found myself for a brief time beginning to explore new and definitely interesting challenges.

I had also experienced original and ground-breaking opportunities most women might not have thought possible for their gender at the time.

These revelations however had left me with a confusing dilemma. Appreciating that although I had now come into possession...in a manner of speaking of interesting deductive and investigative skills I had to come to terms with the reality that there was no longer anyone to share them with. Because of this there would never be any further cause or situation (that I could see) in which to put them to use ever again.

Each year...during the early days of April I set aside some time to carry out what is generally referred to as 'spring cleaning.' For me in particular this means undertaking a series of small to large household tasks in order to make my home spick-and-span from the attic to the ground floor.

Every piece of furniture within the walls of 126 Hill House Road is moved. Any surface within the house that is covered is now uncovered either to be completely dusted or thoroughly cleaned.

This annual spring time routine has now come to include the large writing desk (that had been John's) located in my study where I attend to matters concerning typewriter, pen and paper.

From it the payment of household accounts is seen to, I continue my ongoing correspondence to and from close friends and most importantly in the past it was where my often quickly hand written 'case notes' concerning Sherlock's vocation had been transformed by typewriter into precise detective journals.

I admit that the present condition (mostly due to my overseas vacation) of the surface including the small drawers and pigeon holes of my desk after a time had become - and could be best described in a manner similar as to how John had explained when first seeing Sherlock's desk and study at his cottage in Doncaster...

*(But) he kept his cigars in the coal-scuttle, his tobacco in the toe end of a Persian slipper, and his unanswered correspondence transfixed by a jack-knife into the very centre of his wooden mantelpiece. Thus month after month his papers accumulated, until every corner of the room was stacked with bundles of manuscripts which were on no account to be burned, and which could not be put away save by their owner.*

*What would appear to others as chaos, however, is to my friend a wealth of useful information. Throughout many cases, Holmes would dive into his apparent mess of random papers and artefacts, only to retrieve precisely the specific document or eclectic item he was looking for.*

Rather than allowing myself to become over whelmed with what I was about to undertake I chose instead to follow a very simple and practical approach to the task I had set out for myself. Coming to terms with the 'paper work' (as I thought of it as being) that had accumulated on the desk I would eventually come to create two stacks or collections.

There would first be a discarded collection going to my left that would make its way from my desk and into the wire waste paper basket that was next to me. Then going to my right there would be a saved collection to be filed for the present time then properly dealt with at a later date.

To save time while carrying this out I decided to give only a quick glance at each piece of paper that I would pickup from the desk then determine if it was to make the journey left or right. In the beginning the 'paper work' in front of me consisted mostly of articles of interest that for various reasons I had cut out from daily newspapers to keep.

As well among this particular 'newspaper collection' were saved crossword puzzles from the Times that I had come to enjoy to be solved in my leisure time.

I had shown little or no interest in these acrostic mysteries when John was alive. Later while in Sherlock's company it had been revealed to me that this was one of the more interesting (and less harmful) ways he had found to remain mentally sharp when not involved with a case.

Sherlock had explained this to me in a nonchalant manner "I find the most agreeable and stimulating way to begin my days after finishing breakfast to pour myself a second cup of coffee ...pick up a pencil (or any writing instrument) that is close at hand and decrypt as many of the across and down words contained in the puzzle that I am able to before Mrs. Hudson announces...often in a loud voice from down stairs at the front door that the morning post has arrived."

There were also completed shopping lists and notes reminding me of appointments I had made in the past that had been attended to.

Also among the collection were personal reminders to myself that I had quickly jotted down on the back of empty envelopes. Then there were names and corresponding telephone numbers waiting to be transferred from the paper they were originally recorded on to index cards.

As the 'discarded' collection to my left began to fill the waste paper basket I found myself first quickly looking at...then for a brief time allowing myself to pause from my task...go back and fondly remember in my mind where I was at the time when the various colourful tourist souvenir items...such as brochures, ticket stubs, post cards and photographs I had brought back from my visit to New York City had first come into my possession.

Next just slightly out of my reach…from what seemed like a time so very long ago were the many yellowed with age already opened envelopes each holding either a brief telegram, a personal hand written or formal typed written letter.

My remembrance of each folded piece of paper with in each envelope was like an old photograph that had started to fade with time.

While looking at this collection of most personal correspondence a wave of melancholy washed over me for a moment as I remembered a time when envelopes such as these had been addressed to both John and me then later only I alone receiving such telegrams and letters from Sherlock and his older brother Mycroft.

Already knowing what the contents of each open envelope held and witnessing for a moment the faint long forgotten images and the echoes they were evoking from another time and place I found that I had no wish to dwell upon…or retrace a life for me now over and done with. So I coldly and without acknowledging any emotionlessly dismissed them all and quickly placed them each in turn to my right.

As my desk was now mostly clear of 'paper work' there was only one last article to be dealt with and from its immediate appearance for some present unknown reason that particular piece of paper appeared to have been hastily folded in half.

But as I gazed at it mutely lying there in front of me I suddenly remembered the traumatic nature of its contents. At that point I found myself only wanting to quickly dismiss it and the painful emotions and memories it was recalling in my mind without ever acknowledging it  much less picking it up to unfold and read it again.

I remember the exact time and day at St. Bartholomew's hospital in 1920 when it had first come into my possession.

The attending doctor at the time (a Doctor Lewis) very much at a loss for words while witnessing the growing emotional grief his final sombre pronouncement (concerning John) had just brought about quietly announced while handing me this particular piece of paper."This is only for your records Mrs. Watson"

Taking it reluctantly from his hand…at that very moment I suddenly felt a numbing cold sensation start to spread all through me…and an absolute emptiness come over me…it was as though at that very moment I had been drained of all life with what had just been disclosed.

Almost at once I came to a sudden and overwhelming understanding that the secure and comfortable world I had shared with my loving husband for so many years had been (with only the simple innocent act of receiving the document) suddenly wrenched away from me…so I gave the official notification I had just so blindly taken from the doctor only a cursory glance.

With the chaotic and emotionally troubling state of mind I was finding myself coming to none of the details it contained registered or made any immediate sense to me so in quiet desperation and without thinking I found myself quickly folding it then placing it into my hand bag.

Somehow hoping with this one desperate, futile and certainly empty gesture I could somehow shut out and therefore obliterate the devastatingly emotional life altering event that had just taken place.

---

In my overwhelming grief three years ago and to where I am today I have allowed myself to occasionally go back and relive the few very  precious memories I still have of my final hours and days spent in hospital at my husband's bedside. But as then and now I am troubled by the lack of specific details concerning his death.

Mixed with these memories was and still is the word "indeterminate'' that keeps coming to the front of my mind. It was certainly not a description or explanation that I as a nurse or for that matter anyone in the medical profession would come to expect to read much less accept on any official certificate just below the formal declaration stating 'the cause of death'.

Emotionally settling myself I found the courage to finally unfold and come to terms with what I realized I had been holding onto all this time.

Reading from top to bottom there on a single piece of letter sized whitepaper was laid out the type written cold impartial medical details and detached emotionless statistical information concerning the ending of a life.

However it was that one out of place word that again drew my attention and started me thinking that I might have to bring my dormant investigative skills back into use.

# Chapter 2

I have come to have knowledge of…and also a considerable understanding through professional experience first from John then Sherlock and close personal experience from my writer friend Winifred that death may occur in many ways and forms.

There is of course death by natural causes, sometimes by poisoning (both accidental and deliberate), ill health and occasionally from unforeseen medical complications. There is violent death (as in combat), accidental (unintentional), self-inflicted (suicide) and lastly premeditated death more commonly known of as murder.

Of all the ways to leave or alternatively to be made to leave this mortal world premeditated deaths should be the least likely to occur and the most troubling ones to accept when they do.

This particular type of death most often involves a conscience intent, a single minded conviction, and is often motivated by some blind impulse or purpose.

It is frequently carried out with a certain cold, callous and detached keenness on the part of the person wanting to end a life to follow through with the act from the often much unanticipated or unexpected beginning to the inevitable or fatal end.

With this last cause of death it has been proven all too often that there is rarely any sense of right or wrong involved or even experienced for having carried out the arbitrary act of ending a life.

With these thoughts I put aside my present housekeeping task for a moment...sat back in my chair and looked again at the document in my hand and found myself now seriously questioning the actual cause of John's demise and what had or had not been discovered during his autopsy.

---

An autopsy - also known as a post-mortem examination, is a highly specialized surgical procedure that consists of a thorough examination of a corpse to determine the cause and manner of death and to evaluate any disease or injury that may be present. It is usually performed by a specialized medical doctor known of as a pathologist.

This final medical procedure is performed for either legal or medical purposes. For example, a forensic autopsy is carried out when the cause of death may be a criminal matter, while a clinical or academic autopsy is performed to find the medical cause of death and is used in cases of unknown or uncertain death, or for research purposes.

Chapter 3


My final thought before filing this last document away was that it would be prudent for me to pay a visit to Dr. Norman Lewis on the possibility that he was still in residence at the hospital.

Going back to what I had come to understand and know about autopsies or post mortem examinations was that although he may or may not have performed the procedure this was after all the doctor who had originally given me the document. He there for would be the best person to begin my investigation with.

---

The next morning I telephoned the Fawcett Society...*to explain this is an organisation in the United Kingdom (that I am a member of) that campaigns for women's rights. Its roots date back to 1866, when Millicent Garrett Fawcett dedicated her life to the peaceful campaign for women's suffrage*....being where I spend my week day's volunteering to inform them I would not be available to help that day due to a prior appointment.

Travelling some time and distance from my home by motor taxi I wasn't really appreciating or for that matter even noticing the usual familiar sites passing by as I was being taken to my destination but rather instead I found myself focusing on how best to begin this investigation.

My concentration in this matter was interrupted only by the driver announcing ("St. Bartholomew's hospital Miss") indicating that I had finally arrived at the muted brown sand stone main entrance of a large metropolitan hospital.

This was a location I had not set foot inside of for three years and never imagined I would have any reason to do so again. First paying the fare I then entered the very busy hospital foyer (with patients' doctors and visitors moving about) and made my way to the reception desk to inquire about the doctor.

Preparing myself I confidently inquired "May I please speak with a Doctor Lewis if he is on duty today?" The attendant appeared to gauge me for a moment then responded "I believe he is...may I ask who wishes to speak with him?"

Suddenly feeling what I thought Sherlock might have felt when asked this question for the first time, I confidently answered the attendant with "Mrs. Watson...Mrs. Mary Watson."

As the doctor (whose appearance to me at first glance had changed little since I had last seen him) approached me he wore an expression of puzzlement.

No doubt wondering to himself, with the distance between us closing as to why the widow of a deceased medical doctor after all this time would want to speak with him.

Stopping in front of me and acknowledging me in a professional manner he began the conversation with "Mrs.

Watson...this is certainly an unexpected visit." he then quickly followed with "How may I assist you?"

Reaching into my hand bag I brought out the same piece of paper (now creased) that he had originally given to me. "Doctor Lewis, it is about this" I began as I moved to stand next to him and at the same time I unfolded it then bringing his attention to the section concerning the cause of death. I finished with (while drawing his attention to that particular section) "more specifically it is about this."

Taking it from my hand the doctor (who gave the piece of paper he was now holding a look of recognition) carefully studied it for a moment as if it might (even after all this time) contain some as of yet undiscovered clue.

As he returned it to me I hoped he was about to say the words I had expected to hear but instead (and much to my dismay) replied with only "I'm sorry Mrs. Watson but the cause of your husband's passing away is as much of a mystery now as it was when it occurred three years ago."

Noticing obvious disappointment starting to play across my face Doctor Lewis offered me what he thought might be some spark of hope. Beginning a little uncertainly he said "However...as it happens I do have something from the autopsy which may assist you in solving the cause of his death."

"It is at best a small and probably an insignificant clue that I almost overlooked but decided to keep." With me showing an attentiveness to his forensic contribution he continued "It was found just under the skin in your husband's right hip."

Seeing my expression grow more hopeful he continued "The only reason I took any notice of it in the first place was the bruise that was created where it had entered his body and I wanted to see what may have caused this so I surgically removed it. If you would please wait here Mrs. Watson while I return to my office and I will bring it for you to keep."

Watching as the doctor departed I could only speculate as to what this minor and apparently inconsequential surgical clue was to be.

Shortly as he was returning to me I noticed he was holding in his right hand what appeared to be a small clear cylindrical glass medical vial which (as he got closer) I could see contained a miniature light blue but slightly rusty looking coloured pellet.

Carefully passing it to me like some rare treasure...his face indicating that he was not sure if it was to be of any real assistance I received it sharing much the same thought.

While closely examining the mysterious contents of the glass container and knowing from experience that as a doctor with rounds to attend to my time with him was almost at an end I asked him the obvious question. "Do you believe this may have contributed to John's death?"

The doctor replied "I am not sure...The pellet you are presently holding that was surgically removed from Doctor

Watson showed no residual traces of any poison that might have ended his life neither was there any trace evidence recovered from his body.

There were however puzzling symptoms of a high white blood cell count, damage to the lymph nodes and the haemorrhaging of internal organs and a sore at the site of the bruise."

Placing this somewhat morbid and final remnant of my departed husband along with the medical certificate of death into my handbag I thanked Doctor Lewis for his time and help.

As I was leaving the hospital to hail a motor taxi to return home I realized that I would not be able to immediately make any connection between the pellet I had just received and the cause of John's death on my own. I would have to seek out someone who might have expert knowledge of poisons and the various ways they may be delivered.

Chapter 4

Not sure as to where or even how to begin the investigation…it was during my return journey that I found myself going back in my memory to a time when I had travelled to Gravesend and one possible name and authoritative source of information came to mind.

*When I first heard of Mycroft (through John) I was told that the older brother (of Sherlock) audits books for some government departments, it is later revealed that Mycroft's true role was more substantial. I was never sure of what the brother's exact position was in the British government; it was only commented that "Occasionally he is to the British government the most indispensable man in the country."*

---

*"Three" and Sherlock's third and final finger was raised "I will leave you both (being Winifred and myself) with Mycroft's private office address and his club where he can be contacted and a priority message may be delivered to him immediately should a situation arise that requires my attention here in Gravesend. "If" Winifred gasped…Sherlock continued "If I have gone on to Doncaster, my older brother although an arm chair expert in the arts and skills of detective work will immediately contact me then proceed in my place to expertly assist you (both) until my return."*

As I had found myself returning to a hospital that held bitter sweet memories the next afternoon (again excusing myself from my volunteer duties) I was now returning to a well-remembered government address in another part of the city.

There I hoped to seek the assistance of the one man who had been of great aid to me and to my mystery writer friend when we had needed it most.

Entering the impressive building and after walking a short distance down a green and white linoleum tiled common corridor then turning to my left I opened an office door (which gave no indication of the occupant within) and then made my way into a familiar setting.

It could best be described the most part as an incandescent lit sparsely furnished area with a sturdy office desk and office chair in the foreground.

In the back ground of the room located below a hanging portrait of King George the 5th were five dark green mid-sized metal filing cabinets that were flush to the rear wall and with their backs against the right wall of the outer office were located three plain functional wooden chairs for waiting visitors.

The only distinctive feature of the otherwise austere outer office was a set of polished double oak doors to my left (when facing the rear wall) that lead to an inner office.

As I quietly made my way inside and while looking around I noticed that the only other person present at the moment other than myself was an industrious looking male secretary.

He was seated at the desk (and for the moment unaware of my presence) concentrating on composing a document employing a typewriter.

Looking up and witnessing me now standing directly in front of him the secretary momentarily stopped his task and quietly asked my name and the purpose of my visit. When I answered with both he responded with "Thank you Mrs Watson I will inform Mr Holmes that you have arrived." I was then politely directed to take a seat and asked to wait

As I sat in contemplative silence while studying the afternoon sun light coming in from the office windows that was playing across the unadorned plain pale cream coloured plaster walls I wondered what if any help I might receive this time from Sherlock's older brother concerning my personal matter.

When it seemed that all I would have for company was the constant echoing clatter of a document in progress while I waited the telephone on the desk (to my surprise) suddenly and sharply rang once momentarily stopping the action of type writer keys striking paper.

In response the receiver was briskly picked up by the secretary and placed to his ear...all I heard of the conversation (from him) was a brisk "yes, right away sir."

Returning the receiver back down in its cradle and getting up from behind his desk he stated "please if you will follow me Mrs. Watson, Mr. Holmes will see you now." I was then directed towards the polished double oak doors leading to the inner office.

## Chapter 5

While being escorted from the somewhat plain outer office through the now opened remarkable portals and into a furnished, warm and well-appointed inner office I was again astounded as to the scale of the room of the occupant I was entering.

This indicated to me that the elder Holmes, even after all this time must still be a person of great power, influence and importance.

---

Seeing Sherlock's older brother (smartly attired much as I had remembered him from previous visits) standing beside his commanding desk waiting for me as I entered I was momentarily taken back to earlier times and visits to this same office.

As I approached Mycroft...noticing his distinctive silver grey hair and his perceptive eyes...he warmly smiled at me in recognition, extended his hand in greeting and commented in his familiar gruff voice

"So here we are again Mrs Watson and I understand from your telephone call you have come to see me about something of a personal matter."

Dismissing his secretary ("thank you Jenkins") Mycroft graciously indicated for me to sit in one of the two upholstered chairs that were placed at the front of his desk while he returned to his chair behind the desk.

After seating myself and without displaying any hesitation I started straight away by answering him with "Yes...it concerns my husband and the manner of his death."

Seeing a puzzled look starting to appear on Mycroft's face I silently reached into my hand bag and removed by now two very familiar items. Momentarily standing up from my chair I placed both within his reach and explained (while sitting back down) as I would have to Sherlock "these are the clues."

Taking what had just transpired in stride...Mycroft looked at me for a moment then first picking up the piece of paper in front of him (and unfolding it) he examined John's medical certificate of death. Giving it what I felt was at best only a cursory glance from top to bottom the elder Holmes then offhandedly commented to me "with what I see here it seems to be complete and in order."

Noting my dismayed reaction to his apparently casual observation he quickly scanned the document again then stopped...while still holding it he looked at me again and remarked "ah I think I begin to understand the reason for your coming to see me."

"But you must appreciate that with what I have just read I may be of little help to you in this matter because clinical pathology is an area I have limited if any real expertise in."

Finishing with the document he put it back down then continuing he took up the small clear cylindrical glass medical vial.

Placing it in the fingers of his left and right hand he slowly rotated it horizontally in a clock wise direction while closely studying the small pellet within as it slowly revolved in the same direction.

After a minute or so of concentrating on what he was examining Mycroft returned the vial to its resting place then quietly observed me for a moment.

Obviously seeking clarification of what he had just examined he asked me "and this pellet was surgically removed from your husband?" I silently nodded yes. Showing a sudden awareness in what had just been revealed he commented "this is interesting because this is the second time I have had knowledge of a device similar to this."

Gabriela Paraskeva 1873 – 1922 originally worked as a novelist and playwright in her native east European country then governed by a repressive regime until her defection from that nation in 1920.

After relocating to London, she worked as a journalist for the Times. Miss Paraskeva used this editorial forum to conduct a campaign of sarcastic criticism against the incumbent regime. As a result of this, it had been speculated that the particular countries government may have decided to silence her, and may have asked the Cheka for help.

---

The Cheka was the first of what would become a succession of Soviet state security organizations. It was created on December 20, 1917, after a decree issued by Vladimir Lenin, and was subsequently led by Felix Dzerzhinsky, an aristocrat turned communist. From its founding, the Cheka has proven to be an important military and security arm of the present Bolshevik communist government.

---

Gabriela Sergeyevna Paraskeva aged 49 died as a result of an incident on a London street when a small pellet (coated with a poison that would later be identified as ricin) was injected into her leg with what appeared to be an umbrella wielded by someone associated with that countries secret police.

Returning both the document and the vial to me to put back in my hand bag the elder Holmes to my considerable relief gave me a firm starting point to begin the investigation.

"I am going to suggest you contact a doctor who has a practice in Gravesend. He has seen a pellet similar to yours before so he is most likely to be an expert on this sort of thing and may be able to shed some light as to the cause of your husband's death."

Getting up from behind his desk and then escorting me back to the outer office Mycroft commented "I must admit Mrs Watson this is a curious affair you have brought to my attention. The last time I saw something similar to what you have brought with you today was used to carry out what appeared to be a possible political assassination.

"Although it was never conclusively proven I believe the Cheka" noting my puzzled look at that moment he clarified with "an important military and security arm of the present Bolshevik communist government may have had a hand in it."

"Unless Doctor Watson, your husband had made some dangerous enemies while he was associated with my brother...you and I are at a loss as to why this has taken place."

Before I left Mycroft wrote on an index card the contact information for the doctor he had recommended...that by certain circumstances I had previously met in 1920 on the moving deck of a barge.

# Chapter 6

*Making sure that while Winifred still a little shaky was making her way back to her home I confidently stepped through the large crowd (in Gravesend) that by this time was gathered at the dock.*

*Continuing onto the moving deck of the barge I walked up to the corpse and without any thought asked if I could examine the deceased. The doctor still bent over and concentrating on his task of examination looked up in my direction and sounding a little irritated asked "and you are?"*

*"I am Mary Watson, the widow of Dr. John Watson, I used this opening response hoping that the doctor might make some type of quick connection between myself, John and Sherlock and therefore establish a credible reason for my unusual request.*

*"I assure you that I am a trained nurse. I have seen corpses much worse than this before and only wish to conduct a quick examination of the deceased because I believe there may be a connection between this man and my friend who I have just sent home. "*

*Hearing my assured answer he rose to his feet and immediately extended his right hand in greeting and in a very apologetic voice replied "Mrs. Watson I sincerely apologize...although I did not know your husband personally or as a medical doctor I knew of him and admired him as an excellent chronicler of Mr. Holmes detective cases."*

*After shaking hands with the doctor, whose last name was Briggs he took me into his medical confidence and shared what he had learned from his examination.*

Dr. Michael Briggs – whose parents are Dr George Briggs (retired from the faculty of medicine Imperial College London) and his wife Mrs Catherine Briggs, was born in London in 1896. He completed his medical training in 1917 at Newcastle University with the purpose of becoming a general practitioner.

---

A general practitioner is a medical doctor who treats acute and chronic illnesses and provides preventive care and health education to patients.

General Practitioners intend to practise a holistic approach that takes into consideration the biological, psychological and social environment in which patients live. Their duties are not confined to specific organs of the body, and they have particular skills in treating people with multiple health issues.

With the Great War still raging in Europe Doctor Briggs had attempted to enlist in the army as a front line ambulance orderly but due to a health condition it had rendered him unsuitable for military service.

Deciding instead to broaden his medical experience he immigrated to the Dominion of Canada. There he located a position with a medium sized hospital in the western part of the country and began his internship.

During his residency he came to hear from the returning wounded British soldiers about a small town named Gravesend located in Northwest Kent, England. Making inquiries and finding they did not have a resident doctor he decided he would return to England at the end of the war to set up a modest practice there.

Chapter 7


126 Hill House Road,

London

Dr. Briggs:

On the recommendation of Mr. Mycroft Holmes (by way of introduction the elder brother to Mr. Sherlock Holmes) and for the expert criminal forensic skill you provided to Mr. Sherlock Holmes and myself during the criminal investigation in Gravesend I am seeking your professional medical assistance in revealing the possible cause of my husband's unexplained death. The medical certificate and the cylindrical glass medical vial containing a miniature blue coloured pellet I am sending on to you are the only clues I have to offer.

I would not be writing to you concerning this matter except that Mr. Holmes senior has informed me that you have dealt with a similar article to this before and that you were able to establish both the type of poison used and how it was delivered. While this pending information may or may not help to uncover the person or persons who ended my husband's life it will give me some small comfort and remove the troubling uncertain nature of his death.

Respectfully

Mary N. Watson

Chapter 8

Returning home in the early evening from my busy day of volunteering I was eager to see if a small brown paper wrapped package (similar to the one I had sent) had made its way from 65A Perry Street, Gravesend to 126 Hill House Road, London via the afternoon post.

Removing my hat and coat and hanging them up…then picking up and carrying the much anticipated parcel…it and I made our way into the study. Setting it down in front of me on my desk…I switched on the desk lamp and examined the package for a few minutes not sure as to if or how Dr. Briggs had responded to my unusual request.

Finally deciding to unwrap it to find the answer I located a pair of scissors next to me to cut the twine securing the small box. Carefully slitting the brown wrapping paper covering it I opened it to reveal the contents. First removing the certificate and vial (I had sent) from the packing material within I then took out the letter that had accompanied both. Unfolding it I read the following:

Mrs. Watson:

I am at your service in this matter. To begin Mr. Holmes was correct in that the last time I saw an object similar to the one you have sent was while performing an autopsy on a young woman named Gabriela Paraskeva. Because both Miss Paraskeva and Doctor Watson displayed similar symptoms during their 3 to 5 days of illness after exposure to a toxic substance and each had presented comparable medical evidence during their respective autopsies...in my professional medical opinion the cause of death in both cases was by way of a poison that has been identified as ricin.

---

*Having previous knowledge that I was a trained medical nurse Doctor Briggs with his letter went on to explain the symptoms, nature and delivery of the poison.*

---

The initial symptoms are likely to affect the respiratory system and can include difficulty breathing, shortness of breath, chest tightness, and cough. The symptoms of ricin poisoning are then likely to rapidly progress to include problems such as worsening respiratory symptoms, pulmonary oedema (fluid within the lungs), and eventually, respiratory failure.

As to the unique method of delivery it is a pity that something as beautiful as Delft porcelain was chosen. I came to this conclusion while examining the pellet you had sent noticing its distinctive blue colour.

Although the Delftware potters preferred to call their earthenware "porcelain", it was only a cheaper version of the real Chinese porcelain. Delft Blue was not made from the typical porcelain clay, but from clay that was coated with a tin glaze after it was fired.

As to the method of how the fatal substance may have been fixed to the pellet I can only offer at best some conjecture. It is my belief however that once the ricin was applied there was a second covering of wax or paraffin applied after allowing the pellet to be safely handled.

The pellet now with this protective coating or layer once it had been injected would start melting allowing the poison to slowly be released into the body of the intended person causing a slow and agonizing death. I also believe with this method of delivery there would be no trace of the poison that could be detected during or after an autopsy.

Finally as to how the pellet came to be lodged in the body of both Miss Paraskeva and Doctor Watson? In the case of Dr. Watson due to the nature of the entry wound and subsequent bruising after...it was in all likelihood injected by a high powered spring loaded or compressed air weapon commonly disguised as an umbrella.

It should be noted that you can be exposed to ricin either by ingesting (swallowing) or inhaling (breathing) material containing ricin. In a few rare, past cases, injections of ricin have led to poisoning. This is a very unlikely method of exposure because it requires someone to actually inject the material into you.

However if this particular method of delivery is chosen all that is needed to introduce the poison into an individual would be to stand next to the intended person...gently press the tip of the weapon against them...pull the trigger device...then simply walk away.

I am returning your husband's medical certificate of death and the medical glass vial with a list of possible cities and respective companies where I believe both the pellet and the ricin may have been manufactured. With the information I have provided I hope you will be able to make some connection to both.

Beyond what I have shared with you as a medical doctor I cannot offer any aid in regards as to who may have been responsible for this act and why it has taken place. However if I can be of any further assistance in the matter of your husband's autopsy please do not hesitate to contact me.

Your servant

Dr. Michael Briggs M.D.

Chapter 9

I laid Dr. Briggs response letter down next to the now opened package on my desk and looked up…then out of the large bay window facing east in my study and while watching the stars come out in the evening sky above Hill House Road I began to reflect on what I had just read.

In doing so my mind began to fill with questions first as those of a wife and then as a detective. Some I could possibly address and others alternatively not address.

Recalling what Mycroft Holmes had said in passing as I was leaving his office *"unless Dr Watson had made some dangerous enemies while he was associated with my brother…you and I are at a loss as to why this has taken place"* only added to the difficulty I was about to face.

Starting with the same sound deductive reasoning I had learned from Sherlock I found myself asking three opening questions.

First…was John the intended target…second was he instead a secondary or substitute target in place of Sherlock…or third and the most unlikely had the attack been an unintended mistake? No matter which path I set out to follow all three lead to the same inevitable beginning…who had under taken this and why?

Suddenly I found myself turning and gazing at John's journals on the book shelves lining the study and mentally reviewing all of the case notes my husband had chronicled over the years that I had read many times on my own.

From their content imagining as many probable suspects and scenarios as well as improbable ones to explain the present situation. Then thinking in the end that each one that came to mind was in all likelihood improbable.

I felt that following this route there was to be no possible beginning then I heard a familiar voice of reason say to me..."when you have eliminated the impossible, whatever remains, however improbable, must be the truth".

From that point I knew how I would be spending my evenings at home. After dinner instead of switching on the wireless to listen to a programme presented by the BBC I would sit quietly and comfortably in my arm chair in the parlour.

First turning on a reading lamp then with a cup of tea by my right side I would start from the beginning reading all of John's chronicles. Certainly somewhere in his hand written notes the answer to my problem might be discovered.

# Chapter 10

Deciding I would only study one of John's chronicles each evening I would began with his first "A Study in Scarlett." This was the one in which he establishes himself as the role of chronicler and sets up the narrative stand-point that the work to follow is not fiction, but fact: "Being a Reprint from the Reminiscences of John H. Watson, MD, Late of the Army Medical Department."

The account begins when my husband having returned to London from abroad, runs into an old friend, Stamford, who had been a dresser under him at St. Bartholomew's Hospital.

John confides in Stamford that, due to a shoulder injury that he sustained in a battle during the war he has been forced to leave the armed services and is now looking for a place to live.

Stamford mentions that an acquaintance of his, a Sherlock Holmes, is looking for someone to split the rent at a flat at 221B Baker Street, but he cautions John about the man's eccentricities.

Stamford takes John back to St. Bartholomew's where, in a laboratory, they find Sherlock experimenting with a reagent, seeking a test to detect human haemoglobin. He explains the significance of bloodstains as evidence in criminal trials.

After Stamford introduces John to Sherlock, he shakes my husband's hand and comments, "You have been in battle, I perceive?" Though Sherlock chooses not to explain why he made the comment, John raises the subject of their parallel quests for a place to live in London, and Sherlock explains that he has found the perfect place in Baker Street.

At Sherlock's prompting, the two review their various shortcomings to make sure that they can live together. After seeing the rooms at 221B, they move in and grow accustomed to their new situation.

John is amazed by Sherlock, who has profound knowledge of chemistry and sensational literature, very precise but narrow knowledge of geology and botany; yet knows little about literature, astronomy, philosophy, and politics. Sherlock also has multiple guests visiting him at different intervals during the day.

After much speculation by John, Sherlock reveals that he is a "consulting detective" and that the guests are clients. Facing my husband's doubts about some of his claims, Sherlock casually deduces to John that one visitor, a messenger from Scotland Yard is also a retired Marine sergeant. When the man confirms this, John is astounded by Sherlock's ability to notice details and assemble them.

# Chapter 11

What had started as an undertaking of pure investigative research over the next several evenings was to become a very comfortable way to spend my time before retiring for the night.

There were occasions when it felt that I was all alone in the house with only the company of the mantle clock marking the hours while reading my husband's words. Other times while pausing to gaze lovingly at his picture it was as if John was present sitting with me sharing what he had written so long ago.

With the well-chosen words in his journals, I could almost picture in my mind as to how the professional association and eventual personal friendship between John and Sherlock first began and grew.

While searching for possible clues I came to know more about the man who had become my husband and in turn about the person who had been a mentor first to John then to me.

As my evening project continued I found that with each journal I studied there was still no clue as to his unexplained death. Instead what I was discovering that with my continuing to read page after page there was a growing feeling within me of loss and loneliness for my husband I thought I had finally dispelled from my mind.

Realizing the emotional conflict that was taking place with the investigative course I had chosen I decided that if I could not find what I was seeking in the next journal to be read I would abandon my quest, contact Dr. Briggs to see what further help he might offer.

It was as if fate had played a hand in my next choice to read because I chose John's journal, which he had titled "The Terrible Secret." Here I hoped I would at last uncover a possible clue as to the cause of my husband's death.

# Chapter 12

*It was (as John stated in the narrative) when I gave the details of a series of "by chance" meetings that happened in Zurich between the patent clerk and a person by the name of Margaretha Geertruida "M'greet" Zelle, and the lady in question has been described as a dancer and an entertainer.*

*"If it turns out (Sherlock had replied) it is the same woman then I know her as Mata Hari. Fraulein Zelle adopted her stage name in 1905 in Paris when she started to win fame as an exotic dancer. She poses as a Java princess of priestly Hindu birth, pretending to have been immersed in the art of sacred Indian dance since childhood".*

*"There is a dark side to her that Mr. Einstein may not be aware of. Because the Netherlands remains neutral as a Dutch subject Margaretha Zelle is able to cross national borders freely.*

*To avoid the battlefields, she travels between France and the Netherlands via Spain and Britain and her movements inevitably attract attention. In early 1916, she was travelling by steamer from Spain when her ship called at the English port of Falmouth".*

*"There she was arrested and brought to London where she was interrogated at length by Sir Basil Thomson, Assistant Commissioner at New Scotland Yard in charge of counter-*

*espionage. He gave an account, alleging that she eventually admitted to working for French Intelligence."*

*It is unclear if she lied on this occasion, believing the story made her sound more intriguing, or, if French authorities were using her in such a way, but would not acknowledge her due to the embarrassment and international backlash it could cause.*

*Of course there is some evidence that Mata Hari acted as a German spy and for a time as a double agent for the French, but the Germans had written her off as an ineffective agent whose pillow talk had produced little intelligence of value*

*It should be noted here that Holmes had thoughtfully commented "Circumstantial evidence is a very tricky thing, it may seem to point very straight to one thing, but if you shift your own point of view a little, you may find it pointing in an equally uncompromising manner to something entirely different."*

*The door man knocked on the dressing room door and in response Holmes heard a female voice answer on the other side of the door answer "Oui?" "Un monsieur pour vousvoir mademoiselle". "Come in Pieter"*

*When the lady turned to face her guest and Holmes entered the tiny dressing room there was a look of mutual surprise that passed between them. He for the somewhat revealing costume she was wearing, she for the fact that he was not dressed as a fellow Dutch citizen and therefore could not be Pieter Joost.*

*Turning back to face her dressing room table and mirror Mata Hari picked up the note she had just received and asked "Mr. Holmes?" The next question she framed in a way as if she had no idea of the events that led up to Holmes appearance in her dressing room.*

*"Why is it so important that you have taken great pains to speak to me about information I may, or may not, have? Who is the acquaintance you speak of and what are the consequences of this information falling into the wrong hands?"*

*Holmes sat down in the closest chair and gave Mata Hari a summary of his meetings with Einstein and myself (being John), going into great detail as to the where, why and gravity of the present situation.*

*Picking up her hand bag from the dressing table Mata Hari turned and faced Holmes. She smiled as she opened her hand bag pretending that she was looking for a precious article within.*

*"Mr. Holmes" she started as she changed her gaze from the imagined search of her bag to my friend "what a woman knows in her mind is the same as the contents of a woman's hand bag both are personal and private. She can choose where, when and with whom she desires to share them."*

*It was vain to urge that his time was already fully occupied, for the young lady had decided with some determination not to tell her story, and it was evident that nothing short of force could get her to do so.*

*With Mata Hari's indifferent and somewhat laissez-faire answer, Holmes demeanour and attitude changed. Due to the urgency of the matter Holmes pressed the subject*

*"Mademoiselle it is important that I have an answer to my question." Feeling that she had been boxed in Mata Hari's demeanour and attitude changed as well and then she shot back at him "You are Holmes, the meddler."*

*My friend smiled. "Holmes, the busybody!" His smile broadened. "Holmes, perhaps the Prefecture of Police Jack-in-office!" Holmes chuckled heartily.*

*But seeing no end to this battle of wits, Holmes demeanour changed and he replied "What you have done, or have not done in this world, may be of little or no consequence."*

*"The question becomes what can you make people believe that you have done, or not done?" The brief encounter ended when a back stage employee knocking on Mata Hari's door and announcing "cinq minutes jusqu'àce que voussoyez sur la scène Mademoiselle."*

*Departing from the Moulin Rouge with what he thought of as rare certainty Holmes knew what his next step would be.*

*February 13. Mata Hari was arrested by Captaine Gustave Arnaud of The Prefecture of Policein her room at the Hotel Plaza Athénée in Paris.*

She (Mata Hari) was put on trial, accused of spying for Germany and consequently causing the deaths of at least 50,000 soldiers. Although the French and British intelligence suspected her of spying for Germany, neither (at the time) could produce definite evidence against her.

Her military trial was riddled with bias and circumstantial evidence. Secret ink was found in her room, which was incriminating evidence at the time. She contended that it was part of her make-up.

She wrote several letters to the Dutch Consul in Paris, claiming her innocence. *"My international connections are due of my work as a dancer, nothing else [...]. Because I really did not spy, it is terrible that I cannot defend myself."*

It is probable that French authorities trumped her up as "the greatest woman spy of the century" as a distraction for the huge losses the French army was suffering on the western front.

She was found guilty and was executed by firing squad on 15 October 1917, at the age of 41. Her only real crimes may have been an elaborate stage fallacy and a weakness for men in uniform

---

German documents unsealed later in the 1920s however proved that Mata Hari was truly a German agent. In the autumn of 1915, she entered German service, and on orders of section III B-Chief Walter Nicolai, she was instructed about her duties by Major Roepell during a stay in Cologne.

Her reports were to be sent to the Kriegs nachrichtenstelle West (War News Post West) in Düsseldorf under Roepell as well as to the Agent mission in the German embassy in Madrid under Major Kalle, with her direct handler being Captain Hoffmann, who gave her the code name H-21.

Several of Mata Hari's former lovers held prominent positions in the French military and diplomatic hierarchy. Because of her connections, Colonel Walter Nicolai, head of the German General Staff's intelligence service (Section 3B) regarded Mata Hari as a potentially excellent agent.

Nicolai interviewed her personally in Cologne, but was rather disconcerted when she attempted to seduce him. Despite this, he assigned Mata Hari to gather information from her highly placed friends and lovers in Paris. Adolphe Messimy being one of many was to be the prime target.

Adolphe Messimy Born in Lyon in 1869 was the eldest son of notary Paul Charles Léon Messimy and Laurette Marie Anne Girodon. Messimy graduated from the military school of Saint-Cyr and started a career as a line officer.

When the First World War started Messimy was blamed for the failed French Plan XVII and had to resign on 26 August 1914 because his office going to Alexandre Millerand was the price for a unity government under Viviani.

After his resignation Messimy joined the army as a reserve captain. By 1915 Messimy had been promoted to lieutenant-colonel and on 27 July 1915 he was wounded in the Vosges, leading a unit of Chasseurs Alpins.

Promoted to colonel, he was given command of the 6th brigade of chasseurs. Wounded again on 4 September 1916 on the Somme, Messimy was promoted to general de brigade on 11 September 1917 and transferred to command the 213th brigade of infantry.

---

# Chapter 13

Continuing with John's journal.

*(Sherlock wrote...) I must first start by profoundly apologizing to you both (Sherlock meaning John and I) for not returning to London after my time in Paris.*

*As you have no doubt already read in the newspapers the eventual fate of Margaretha Geertruida "Margreet" Zelle or Mata Hari. You have known from past cases Watson, whenever I have handed over a criminal into the custody of the police there was never any doubt that I was serving the law and that this was the right action to take.*

*However, with the case of Mata Hari there will always be some doubt as to whether she was in fact a genuine German spy who could have caused great harm, or if in fact, because of her career, only believed that she was a spy and held the idea she was capable of extracting important secrets from the men who came into her life while she was an exotic entertainer.*

*In either case, it's a wicked world when a clever woman turns her brain to what she may believe is a crime. That is the worst of all."*

*Once or twice in my career I feel that I have done more real harm by my discovery of the criminal than ever he or she had done by his or her crime. I thought I had learned caution now, and I should have rather played tricks with the law of the land than with my own conscience."*

---

With reading this last paragraph of the chronicle I felt that if I could arrange it I would set out and search for all the people who may have had any association with this supposed exotic spy. While investigating I also intended to find out if she or any of her romantic assignations were in any way connected to John's death.

But I had a suspicion that if I undertook such an examination it would be revealed that there would be certain respectable individuals within our government and other governments who, with what had taken place may have wanted Sherlock's or for that matter John's death to come about for reasons best known only to them.

This questionable course may have been a plot with the purpose of eliminating one person to further the ambitions of others. However I definitely intended to follow up on Dr. Briggs list by writing to the various companies in the suggested countries that dealt with the manufacture of porcelain and poison. There was a slight chance they might reveal the person or persons who had brought the two into a lethal combination.

Whether by chance or coincidence I came across this article I had cut out (and saved) from a newspaper some time ago.

---

During the raid on the home of a man and son located in Brixton January 1920, a very small amount of ricin was allegedly found in a sealed jam jar kept in a kitchen cupboard. A father and son, Jack and Nicky Davidson were arrested under the War Emergency Laws (Continuance) 1920 Act.

The arrests followed a long-running police led investigation against the German Workers Party which is presently involved in extreme right-wing political activity in Germany and in the United Kingdom.

Jack Davidson was sentenced to ten years in May 1920, for preparing acts of hostility, three counts of possessing material useful to commit acts of violence and possessing a prohibited weapon; his son was given two years for possessing material useful to commit acts of violence.

# Chapter 14

Prime Minister Willem Bastiaan van Steenwyk, OM, CH, ED, KC, FRS PC (born 24 May 1870) is a prominent South African and British Commonwealth statesman, military leader and philosopher. In addition to holding various cabinet posts, he served as Prime Minister of the Union of South Africa. He is a supporter of racial segregation and white minority rule in this African country.

---

I would learn of this man for the sinister and treacherous acts he had undertaken during the First World War...for his far reaching course of action following the armistice and of his uncaring and callous actions undertaken during the Rand Rebellion.

---

The Rand Rebellion was an armed uprising of white miners in the Witwatersrand region of South Africa, in March 1922. Jimmy Green, a prominent politician in the Labour Party, was one of the leaders of the strike.

Following a drop in the world price of gold from 130 shillings (£6 10s) a fine troy ounce in 1919 to 95s/oz. (£4 15s) in December 1921, the companies tried to cut their operating costs by decreasing wages, and by weakening the colour bar to enable the promotion of cheaper black miners to skilled and supervisory positions.

The rebellion started as a strike by white mineworkers on 28 December 1921 and shortly thereafter, it became an open rebellion against the state. Subsequently the workers, who had armed themselves, took over the cities of Benoni and Brakpan, and the Johannesburg suburbs of Fordsburg and Jeppe.

The young Communist Party of South Africa (CPSA) took an active part in the uprising on grounds of class struggle while opposing racist aspects of the strike, which were typified by the slogan; "*Workers of the world unite and fight for a white South Africa!*"

Several communists, including the strike leaders Percy Fisher and Harry Spendiff, were killed as the rebellion was quelled by state forces. The rebellion was eventually crushed by "considerable military firepower and at the cost of over 200 lives".

Prime Minister van Steenwyk crushed the rebellion with 20,000 troops, artillery, tanks, and bomber aircraft. By this time the rebels had dug trenches across Fordsburg Square and the air force tried to bomb but missed and hit a local church. However the army's bombardment finally overran them.

---

During the First World War, van Steenwyk had formed the South African Defence Force. His first task was to suppress a rebellion, which was accomplished by November 1914. While the campaign went fairly well, the German forces involved were not destroyed.

Van Steenwyk was criticised by his chief Intelligence officer, Colonel Richard Meinertzhagen, for avoiding frontal attacks which, in Meinertzhagen's view, would have been less costly than the inconsequential flanking movements that prolonged the campaign where thousands of Imperial troops died of disease.

As for van Steenwyk, Meinertzhagen wrote: "van Steenwyk has cost Britain many hundreds of thousands of lives and many millions of pounds by his (assumed) caution...van Steenwyk was never an astute soldier; a brilliant statesman and politician but no soldier."

However he was promoted to honorary lieutenant general for distinguished service in the field on 1 January 1917. Early in 1917van Steenwyk left Africa and went to London as he had been invited to join the Imperial War Cabinet and the War Policy Committee by Prime Minister David Lloyd George

---

It should be noted like most British Empire political and military leaders in World War I, van Steenwyk thought the American Expeditionary Forces (who had entered the war in 1918) lacked the proper leadership and experience to be effective quickly. He supported the Anglo-French amalgamation policy towards the Americans.

In particular, he had a low opinion of General John J. Pershing's (the general officer of the United States Army who led the American Expeditionary Forces in World War I) leadership skills.

So much so that he wrote a confidential letter to David Lloyd George proposing Pershing be relieved of his command and that the US forces be placed "under someone more confident, like himself". This did not endear him to the Americans once it was leaked.

Chapter 15

My only experience of armed conflict up until this time had come solely from my husband. This being John relating his experiences as a medical doctor of a hospital...his chief duty had been to attend to the terribly wounded soldiers returning home from combat at the front.

My only other experience came (albeit vicariously) from noticing the brash and boldly published war related headlines.

Each expressed below the banner of the respective daily newspapers that were collectively and prominently displayed by outdoor news agent shops located throughout the city in hope of catching the attention of pedestrians as they walked by.

My, as well as The Fawcett Society members experience of armed conflict would be considerably broadened when the plight of Susan Fisher and Emily Spendiff, the widows of Percy Fisher and Harry Spendiff (the strike leaders killed during the Rand Rebellion) came to our attention.

During the later stages of the Rebellion, the South African Defence Force pursued the policy of rounding up and isolating the civilian population in concentration camps, one of the earliest uses of this method by modern powers.

Women and children were sent to these camps. A report after the rebellion concluded that 27,927 (of whom 22,074 were children under 16) and 14,154 black Africans had died of starvation, disease and exposure in the camps.

Although the government had comfortably won the parliamentary debate by a margin of 252 to 149, it was stung by the criticism and concerned by the escalating public outcry, and called on Willem Bastiaan van Steenwyk for a detailed report.

In response, complete statistical returns from camps were sent in July 1922. By August 1922, it was clear to government and opposition alike that their worst fears were being confirmed – 93,940 women and children and 24,457 black Africans were reported to be in "camps of refuge" and the crisis was becoming a catastrophe as the death rates appeared very high, especially among the children.

The government responded to the growing clamour by appointing a commission. The Fawcett Commission, as it would become known was, uniquely for its time, an all-woman affair headed by Millicent Fawcett who despite being the leader of the women's suffrage movement was a Liberal Unionist and thus a government supporter and considered a safe pair of hands.

Between August and December, 1922, the Fawcett Commission conducted its own tour of the camps in South Africa. While it is probable that the British government expected the Commission to produce a report that could be used to fend off criticism, in the end it confirmed everything that Emily Hobhouse (one of the members of the commission) had said. Indeed, if anything the Commission's recommendations went even further.

The Commission insisted that rations should be increased and that additional nurses be sent out immediately, and included a long list of other practical measures designed to improve conditions in the camp. Millicent Fawcett was quite blunt in expressing her opinion that much of the catastrophe was owed to a simple failure to observe elementary rules of hygiene.

Chapter 16


Pausing my research of John's journals for a time because of the remembered newspaper article concerning Jack and Nicky Davidson's arrest I decided to reread the reply letter (regarding the pellet) Dr. Briggs had sent to me.

---

*"I am returning the medical certificate of death and the glass vial with a list of possible cities and respective companies where I believe both the pellet and the ricin may have been manufactured. With the information I have provided I hope there will be some connection between the listed cities and manufacturers."*


---


Realizing that taking on the daunting task of writing to all the companies the doctor had brought to my attention would take far more time than I had available I turned again to the one person who would be of help.

I was confident that he would have the necessary resources and personnel to write to the listed cities and respective companies to see if they were or had been engaged in the manufacturer of porcelain and poison.

After contacting him by telephone and making a request for assistance Mycroft offered "I will have my personal secretary Jenkins come to your home to pick up the list.

Leave it with me for a few days Mrs. Watson and I will see what my office can find out about these companies for you." Then as much to me as to himself he finished the conversation with "I believe I will start with Hewlett's Industrial directory for the United Kingdom and Europe."

A week later the person who had initially come to the house to pick up Dr. Briggs list returned with the same which I noticed it had now been extensively annotated.

While it catalogued some North American as well as some European companies as possible manufacturers of ceramic pellets there was a noticeable absence of information as to where the poison may have originated from leaving me unable to connect the two.

At the bottom of the list I noticed there was a personal hand written foot note from Mycroft...

*"To finish Mrs. Watson in the 17th century, Royal Delft had several factories all over Delft. However, this was very inconvenient and in 1916 all of their activities were centralised in the location which is still the current visiting address of the factory, at the Rotterdamseweg in Delft, Holland.*

*Interestingly, and maybe a bit unusual is that one of my staff also located a delft factory that was engaged in the manufacture of munitions during the war which I believe in some way may be associated to the van Steenwyk family. It is known by the Dutch name of Loosdrechts which is located in Selby an industrial district in the South African city of Johannesburg."*

*Mycroft*

Chapter 17

I had not been a part of the original Fawcett commission that had toured the concentration camps which by some had been euphemistically referred to as 'camps of refuge' in The Union of South Africa between August and December 1922.

The personal reasons I gave (to any one inquiring) for wanting to go to South Africa was to follow in the steps of the commission by taking the journey on my own.

While there I wished first to conduct a follow up inspection of the camps and then talk more with Susan Fisher and Emily Spendiff the widows of the Rand Rebellion.

With these stated intentions my explanation would be sound and plausible if anyone should question at any length my reason for leaving the United Kingdom for a short time.

From what I had learned from Mycroft the actual purpose for my trip was far more personal. Having already arranged train travel to Dover and ocean passage across to the African continent with reserving a room (under my maiden name) at the Monarch Hotel located in Rosebank, a prestigious suburb of Johannesburg all that was needed was an invitation to a gala ball. Which I very much hoped would be attended by van Steenwyk where an opportunity could present its self to be asked by him for a waltz.

While travelling through the quiet night time lit streets of Johannesburg by taxi cab on my way from my hotel to an evening social event taking place at the Pretoria Hotel I again opened the envelope and looked at the engraved invitation (that had been anonymously delivered to my hotel).

It read I would be attending (as an invited guest at the request of Willem Bastiaan van Steenwyk) the annual ball held in celebration of The Battle of Spion Kop.

---

*The Battle of Spion Kop was fought about 24 miles west-south-west of Ladysmith on the hilltop of Spioen kop along the Tugela River, in Natal province South Africa from January 23 to 24 1900. It was fought between the South African Republic and the Orange Free State on the one hand and British forces during the Second Boer War it was a campaign during the war to relieve Ladysmith. It was a British defeat.*

---

I stood unaccompanied (dressed in an elegant blue evening gown) at the darkened curtained entrance to the grand sparkling crystal chandelier lit ballroom while awaiting my formal introduction...this is the custom at occasions such as this.
Parting the dark heavy draped curtains slightly and stepping forward for a moment I briefly looked in and viewed all the sights and took in all the sounds of the gala ball taking place within.

What I beheld was a vast well-appointed chandelier lit room almost to overflowing with elegantly dressed and formally attired couples all dancing together in time to a familiar Strauss waltz.

With the last rousing notes of the Emperor waltz fading into the air there was a pause for appreciative applause from all the waltzing couples and guests.

As I was silently being directed to come through the entrance the maestro conducting the orchestra noticed me then spoke into the microphone formally announcing to all in attendance. "Ladies and gentlemen introducing Miss Mary Morstan from London in the United Kingdom."

While I was making my entry into the bright and spacious room I noticed that there was the occasional curious glance given in my direction. While passing by those in attendance my presence was accompanied to the sound of polite light applause.

When I was of no further interest to anyone in the room I quickly and inconspicuously made my way across the now empty polished parquet ball room floor to an unoccupied chair which was located by the wall opposite to the entrance.

While comfortably seating myself and appreciating the sophisticated atmosphere surrounding me I felt assured and confident that I would now finally have my chance to bring the quarry (van Steenwyk) to account. I fully intended to take advantage of any opportunity that should present its self during the evening.

While in his company I would be bold as I asked the questions that I needed answers to. I assured myself that I would be safe undertaking this task knowing while he and I were being observed by other couples no action would be taken against me and that I should not come to any harm.

Although I had no idea as to his exact appearance as I casually listened to bits of passing conversations and at the same time searched all the faces of the people moving about in the room I was confident that somehow I would recognize him long before he would recognize me.

But as I was returning my gaze to what was directly in front of me I heard a strongly accented Boer (the descendants of the Dutch who had settled in the country that would one day be known as the Union of South Africa) male voice to my immediate right announce in a commanding manner that required no reply.

"Good evening Miss Morstan or I should more properly address you as Mrs. Watson...please allow me to introduce myself I am Willem Bastiaan van Steenwyk. I am pleased you accepted my invitation to attend the ball this evening and I should like to have this next waltz with you?"

Momentarily caught off guard with this sudden development (and the apparent knowledge of my identity) I shifted my gaze to the direction the voice had originated from.

Looking up for a moment at the gentleman formally dressed in a tuxedo now boldly presenting himself to me I shockingly realized that the man who had just made the demanding request was quite possibly a suspect in John's death.

While trying to regain my composure from the initial jolt I had experienced I heard myself (almost as if an entirely another person) blindly reply to him "yes" without thinking of any possible repercussions of my decision.

As the familiar opening strains (being played by French horns and the violins) of The Blue Danube waltz began to play and we were making our way out and onto the ball room floor...with this wholly unexpected turn of events I watched with some regret as all my cleverly thought out plans began to slip away behind me like sand flowing out from the bottom of a broken hour glass.

With the stirring notes of the orchestral music building and then filling the vast room and as we began the waltz together in and amongst the company of the other couples on the ball room floor my mind suddenly went blank and I could not think of any of the questions I had so confidently expected to ask.

To break the growing awkward silence between us my dance partner inquired…and not in the manner of polite conversation or general curiosity but rather as a question posed in the threatening manner a powerful lion exhibits as it begins to hunt its prey.

"And what brings you to Johannesburg Mrs. Watson?" Not sure if I was going to be giving away what little advantage I might still retain I found myself quickly replying in a nonchalant manner with what I knew to be a totally fictitious answer "to visit with family".

And although he did not come out and state that he had found my weak attempt at an answer both lacking and somewhat transparent his expression implied that he wanted to know more.

Before I had any chance to carefully think through a more substantive (yet safe) reply I heard myself without any thought or caution follow up with "and to visit a delft factory I have heard of which I believe is located somewhere in Selby an industrial district of this city."

Suddenly I realized with that revealing answer I had now put myself in a potentially dangerous position. While trying to concentrate on the rhythm of the waltz and mask my growing dread I waited anxiously and with some trepidation to hear what his response might be.

Observing his immediate reaction I could tell that my statement had been unexpected and that the former prime minister was no doubt thinking of several different ways to acknowledge it.

In a panic at that moment I found myself suddenly wanting to quickly retract my rash answer with an "Excuse me but my mind must have been elsewhere for a moment."

But before I could get those words out to my considerable surprise and relief he obliquely answered with a deflecting response of "are you thinking of starting a delft collection or are you adding to an existing one?"

Realizing that I had unexpectedly been presented with an opportunity in which I might pursue at least part of one of my questions I cryptically started my reply (having already gained knowledge from Dr. Briggs) with "I have recently acquired an interest in delft porcelain and wanted to know more about it.

While I am in Johannesburg I thought I might visit the factory." Then drawing on my inner courage I finished with "Do you perhaps know the name and the directions as to how to get there?"

Just as I thought I was about to acquire some valuable information regrettably I heard the final notes of the waltz being played.

With the music ending and while witnessing couples now slowly leaving the ball room floor to return to their seats I suddenly found that my dance partner was quickly excusing himself.

"I do not wish it to appear that I am rushing away Mrs. Watson...and I would enjoy another waltz with you...but I have matters that need attending to. So I will wish you a good evening and I hope you will enjoy the rest of your visit to Johannesburg and perhaps we shall meet again."

Wondering at that moment if maybe I had struck a nerve with that unusual departure I watched as the former military leader and philosopher Willem Bastiaan van Steenwyk quickly depart from the still much occupied ball room to retrieve his hat and evening coat from the check room.

From his hurried exit into the night I had some suspicion that he was soon going to be sharing the contents of our brief waltz conversation with others who may have had an interest in my visit.

# Chapter 18

Loosdrechts Porselainas the factory is known is located at 437 Booysen Road off of Main Reef Road in Selby, an industrial district of the city.

It is a sizeable yet unassuming one story weathered white brick building. Despite the descriptive sign located next to where the factory delivery vans arrive and depart from…the building's functional construction and general appearance gave no indication as to the military manufacturing purpose it had served during the Great War.

---

After paying the fare and dismissing the taxi cab I looked about until I located a sign that would direct me to an entrance. Almost in front of me I saw a functional looking door bearing the precisely hand lettered words indicating "Main Office" in English and "Hoofdkantoor" in Afrikaans.

Not sure as to what my next step in the investigation would be I realized as I was making my way inside the building and to the customer reception area I was going to have to create a believable, convincing character and role in order to acquire further information regarding the manufacture of delft porcelain .

I decided I would pose as a professional business woman engaged in possible mercantile trade with this manufacturer of ceramic goods and not as a mere female entering a

London department store to casually browse their Wedgewood figurines to complete her collection.

---

"Good afternoon madam…my name is Marius Bakeberg may I be of any assistance?" queried the gentleman I turned to see entering the reception area just after I had.

From his immediate presence and professional manner I quickly took him to be either the managing director or someone in authority with the company.

Knowing that I could not reveal my actual intentions for the visit my answers would have to be somewhat general in nature and yet at the same time hopefully pique his interest.

Taking on my new persona I confidently answered "Yes I am seeking a ceramic manufacturer who may assist the company I am employed with to develop a specialized product."

With a mixture of both professional interest and at the same time caution he inquired "And what type or kind of product might this be?"

Knowing that I did not have a ready supply of well thought out replies to his question I quickly and bravely responded with "small delft porcelain pellets." Of course before going any further I was tempted to enquire if this question had been posed by anyone to him before.

As if trying to probe the nature of my request his answer was somewhat elusive in nature. "Delft porcelain may take on many shapes or forms and serve many purposes...from functional to decorative."

"Pellets"...here he thoughtfully paused for a moment then continued ..."would not be a common use for something so beautiful unless they were to be used to make...perhaps an enchanting necklace?"

"But I assume you did not come to Loosdrechts Porselain seeking material to manufacture mere costume jewellery." Giving me what I took to be a knowing look he continued with "Perhaps you are seeking a more *practical* use for our product?"

With those words spoken I hoped that I had attained the purpose of my visit. However I assessed the person standing in front of me then realized I had reached an impasse.

I weighed the answer I wanted to give in regards to the manner of John's death there by possibly revealing the actual intention of my visit and my identity but lose a valuable lead.

Or I could give a fictitious answer that would serve at best to reveal if this company had in the past manufactured small delft porcelain pellets capable of delivering poison and not reveal who I was.

Crossing my fingers in my mind I confidently replied "my company supplies various types of materials used in industrial polishing machines." Seeing that my opening statement required some explanation I continued…"material such as silica and fine sand"…not sure if I was being believed or not I carried on with "also small glass and metal beads".

Realizing I had now reached the point as to where I was stretching the very bounds of credibility I finished with "and now possibly ceramic beads or pellets that are manufactured by your company."

With that the business-related conversation came to a sudden and unexpected halt when instead of receiving any conformation that I had found a connection I was instead pointedly asked "Excuse me but I do not remember if I asked or if you gave me your name and the name of the company you are employed with when we first met."

Realizing that with my presence in Johannesburg and at the gala ball the previous evening my name and its many possible associations would already be well known to a select few…with apologies to John and Sherlock I convincingly gave my name as Mrs. Adler…Mrs. Irene Adler.

Hoping that the person who had just posed this question was not too well versed about the names of British manufacturers

I gave the first business name that came to mind being Courtin and Warner as my employer.

Although not being sure if he was fully persuaded with the information that I had just provided him my visit to Loosdrechts Porselain located at 437 Booysen Road off of Main Reef Road in Selby had ended.

With a certain cold finality it concluded with a cynical "Mrs. Adler" there was a slight pause in his closing statement…indicating a lack of believability as to the identity I had just given."If you will please give me the name of the hotel you are staying at I will get word to you shortly as to whether my company and your employer will be able to conduct any business."

Chapter 19

Later that day as I was walking through the Monarch hotel lobby I noticed there were only a few seated guests present(some talking together others engaged with newspapers) as I made my way past them to the front desk to ask for my room key and to see if there were any messages waiting for me.

"Good afternoon Miss Morstan" the smartly attired desk clerk cheerily greeted me "I trust you had a pleasant day today." I smiled and answered "yes I did and may I have the key to my room please?"

While handing the key to me I noticed that a small envelope bearing only the name of the hotel was also being passed across the desk...this action finished with the desk clerk stating "this note just came for you."

Thinking that it was too soon for a reply from the delft porcelain factory I decided it might be from either Mycroft or Dr. Briggs. With both the key and the unaddressed mail now in my possession curious as to who the sender was...I went and sat in a red leather wing back chair close to the front desk.

Going back to my initial suspicion...today's event confirmed that when I did undertake an examination I was now discovering that there were certain (as of yet unknown) individuals who may in fact have had a hand in the matter I was investigating for reasons best known only to them...the envelope I was now holding onto which I was about to read would soon confirm this

Setting the room key down on a small table to my left I slit open the envelope using my nail file and removed the contents. Instead of the expected folded piece of paper in its place there was only a small card of the same dimensions as a place holder that is used at formal dinner settings.

But unlike a place holder there was no first or last name engraved on it only the quickly hand written words *"Mrs. Watson...some events and the people involved in them are better left undisturbed."*

---

Like the unforeseen card there was an unexpected letter that had arrived from Gravesend awaiting my return to London. It's revealing contents holding some promise of bringing me one step closer to connecting the delft porcelain pellet to the fatal powder it had been coated with.

---

Chapter 20

65A Perry Street,
Gravesend

Mrs. Watson:

Further to my previous letter regarding the particular toxic
material that was used to take your husband's and Miss
Paraskeva's life I decided to go back to examine it in more
detail and conduct further research.

To this end I consulted Medical Chemistry and Toxicology
James William Holland 3rd edition. Casarett&Doull's
Toxicology 2nd edition. Medical Toxicology, Principles of
Toxicology Edited by G. Lestrade and a Textbook of
Medical Jurisprudence and Toxicology Dr. Jaising P. Modi.
All confirm ricin's method of extraction, chemical
composition and terminal effects on the human body.

Each text corroborates that castor beans are processed
throughout the world to make castor oil. Ricin is part of the
waste "mash" produced when castor oil is made.

Once the substance is extracted (with the chemical acetone)
it can then be produced in the form of a powder (possibly in
Dr. Watson's case that was used to coat the porcelain pellet),
a mist, or a solid pellet, which can be dissolved in water or
weak acid.

It is a stable substance under normal conditions but can be inactivated by heat above 80 degrees centigrade (176 degrees Fahrenheit).

Although no approved therapeutics are currently based on ricin, it has been shown to have the potential to be used in the treatment of tumours, as a so-called "magic bullet" to destroy targeted cells.

Again Ricin is a toxic substance found naturally in castor beans. If castor beans are chewed and swallowed, the released poison can cause injury.

I cannot attest as to the accuracy or reliability of the information I am about to pass onto you Mrs. Watson concerning one particular manufacturer of this toxic substance. It is based solely on conversations I came to hear from the returning sick and wounded Allied soldiers who were in my care.

The men repeatedly spoke of seeing, as they over ran the German trenches in Ypres was a company name stencilled in white letters on the sides of empty wooden crates that the gas shells or canisters had been delivered to the trenches in…the name was Metzger Chemische.

Chapter 21

The Great War exacted a terrible toll on all the nations who had been involved in the global conflict. None was greater than the toll that had been inflicted on one particular city of the German nation.

---

The city of Dresden is located in a valley on the River Elbe, near the Czechoslovakian border. It has a long history as the capital and royal residence for the Electors and Kings of Saxony, who for centuries furnished the city with cultural and artistic splendour. The city was known as the Jewel Box, because of its baroque and rococo city centre.

---

I had initially travelled the long rail journey from the French port of Calais primarily to follow up on the information Dr. Briggs had supplied (in his latest letter) concerning a possible German manufacturer of the poison that had taken my husband's life. Secondarily in spite of the extensive damage from allied aerial bombing I hoped to take what remained of the famed beauty of this city.

From the moment I left my passenger carriage (being one in a long train of many) on the Deutsche Reischbahn (loosely translated) the German National Railway train I had journeyed on across Europe I found I was now making my way through a cavernous, cold and certainly much deserted Dresden Hauptbahnhof or main railway station.

An unpleasant conclusion was starting to form in my mind that with each step I took that I was entering a terribly bleak, and disturbingly uncertain world. One of bitterness over the conditions of hyperinflation…total devastation…mass starvation…homelessness…and general political upheaval all the result of a futile war.

Stopping to ask someone I took to be a Bahnhof porter or station porter in broken German for directions to my hotel I found that it was only a short distance from the train station. I casually remarked in passing that it would then be more expedient for me to walk there instead of hiring transportation.

The answer I received in turn was an emphatic "fraulien wares sicherer fur Ihr Hotel anstatt zu Fußfahren" with what little German I could understand his answer informed me it would be in my best interests to signal a taxi to stop and take me and my luggage to my destination.

While at home planning my journey I had come to overhear rumours, read in foreign newspapers stories of 'Deutschlands Niederlage!'–'Germany in defeat!' and see pictures of a down trodden and defeated population accompanying the news accounts.

Men, women and children all mutely standing together in endless lines or queues to obtain the staples of life from outdoor soup kitchens. Their resigned and endless waiting resulting in only one meagre daily meal consisting of stale bread and a thin soup.

This dreadful reality was played out before me city block after city block during my short ride from the station. The sight of lost, pale and pallid faces that passed on each side of the passenger windows of the taxi had persuaded me when I arrived to stay at my hotel and venture out only when necessary.

Although only six years had passed since the end of the War most of Dresden was still spiritually and structurally devastated and in ruins. It felt as if its residents…long weary of battles won or lost had given up all hope of ever rebuilding their own lives and rebuilding the life of their once beautiful city.

Chapter 22

Upon my arrival at the Hotel zum Nussbaum (a modest guesthouse situated in the quiet residential suburb of Briesnitz) and while confirming my reservation I was grateful to hear that the Rezeption Schreiber or front desk clerk spoke German accented English. This would make the task I had come to this city for far easier to undertake.

Hoping to maintain my anonymity for as long as I was able to when he requested…"and sign your full name here please Fraulein" while registering I again gave my last name as Morstan.

I thought it wise still not to use my married last name or Irene Adler (the name I had used while in Johannesburg) on the chance there were those in Germany who had read translated editions of the Strand Magazine and could make some possible association to either name.

---

The chemical and pharmaceutical sector came to Dresden at the end of the 19th century. There is P and W Verpackungen and Metzger Chemische (manufacturers of mustard gas and ricin). The Sächsisches Serumwerk Dresden (Saxon Serum Plant, Dresden), owned by a major British drug manufacturing company, a world leader in pharmaceutical production. Another traditional producer is Arzneimittelwerke Dresden (Pharmaceutical Works, Dresden).

Herr Albrecht Metzger - Director of Metzger Chemisch located at 437 Grunaer Strasse was born, raised and educated in Dresden Germany. He had served in the army in the First World War as a Captain in the 3rd Landwehr division.

---

"Guten Morgen...Bitte entschuldigen Sie...please my apologies...Good morning Fraulein Morstan...my name is Albrecht Metzger and I am the director of Metzger Chemisch. Welcome to the company and also to the city of Dresden."

# Chapter 23

The man who had provided me with my invitation and was now formally greeting me at the front entrance I would have to describe as being both charming and hospitable. He was a little above average in height and of a thin build and features.

With short sandy brown hair that was starting to turn grey and arresting glacier blue eyes I thought him to be between 40 to 45 years of age.

Despite wearing a smartly tailored business suit as one would expect the director of a chemical company to be Herr Metzger retained and displayed a distinct military presence about him.

As we were making our way in from the entrance through the lobby then while ascending a broad stair case leading to an airy carpeted hall that would take us to his spacious office he commented to me.

"You have arrived at just the right time Fraulein Morsten…breakfast (I hope you have not already eaten) has already been served and now that I have your company it will be a much more pleasant meal."

Entering the administrative area of the company he directed me towards a dinette table already set for two…the table (with two chairs) being thoughtfully located near to a wide ceiling to floor window offering a panoramic morning (undamaged) view of the city.

The pleasant aroma of the meal awaiting us is known of in Europe as a continental breakfast. While sitting down and before eating...somehow feeling that I should set the course and pace of the morning appointment I began with "this is certainly an unexpected pleasure Herr Metzger. I will certainly try to ask only a few questions and not take up too much of your time."

Smiling at my polite opening comment as he poured my first cup of coffee the director graciously replied "Please do not feel that you must rush off Fraulein...my company leaves me to myself during the morning and only makes great demands of me in the afternoon."

"Besides I found your letter to be most compelling and I will certainly try to share with you all that I know as to how our company manufactures castor oil and *medicinal* ricin."

Passing the now filled cup with saucer to me he asked "do you take milk and sugar?"

The leisurely meal in the warm morning sun lit office was enjoyed by us both in an atmosphere of mutual and comfortable silence.
It was only when I thought it an appropriate moment during the course of breakfast that I chose to pose a few of what I

thought to be of general interest questions…this had been my subtle way of testing the waters.

Hoping that the director's guard might now be lowered a little and while appearing to fix my attention on only buttering another piece of toast for myself I casually brought up one of my major concerns.

Trying to sound nonchalant and not really too interested I inquired "and what is done with the waste 'mash' material after the castor oil is produced and the medicinal ricin is extracted?"

With that question the director unexpectedly put down his fork and knife and gave me an expression that he had suddenly been taken unaware.

First composing himself while slowly picking up his fork and knife then resuming the meal…without being looked at or spoken to directly…I found I was now confronted with the somewhat cold tone of voice and unexpected display of military authority the type an officer only employs when redressing a subordinate.

"If you do not mind my asking Fraulein Morsten (here he paused) how did you become interested in ricin in the first place?"

Knowing that this subject would surface soon after my arrival at the chemical company with the scenario I had created in my mind while on the long rail journey from Calais to Dresden I began...

---

Of course while anticipating this situation I originally reasoned rather than launch into some long and elaborate explanation instead I entertained the thought of setting a simple but effective trap using thinly disguised terrible events I had gone through with John as a lure.

With the trap baited then sprung and escape quite impossible I would then confront the guilty party with the gathered facts. This plan was to have unfolded in aid of quickly extracting a full confession and an admission of guilt.

---

But as in Johannesburg I did not wish to put at risk or damage any possible source of information with such an audacious plan.

With what I had just experienced I decided on a safer approach. That being the 'uncle' I had mentioned in my inquiry letter who had died in hospital of an inoperable tumour and I had only come to learn of ricin and its ability to specifically cure damaged tissue after.
But (to myself) I hoped that during the course of the morning visit I might inadvertently learn more of the sinister nature of ricin.

Chapter 24

Appearing to be somewhat placated with my reply the director regained his composure and sincerely replied "My condolences to you Fraulein"…then after a short pause while placing his coffee cup back down on its saucer he announced "when you have finished breakfast we shall begin the tour."

With the morning meal ended we got up from the table and together left his office. After a short walk through the administrative wing of the building and lastly passing through a set of double doors I in the company of the director had left a quiet and hushed atmosphere and now found ourselves standing on the very busy, noisy and extensive factory floor that was the heart of Metzger Chemisch.

Herr Metzger stood silently and slightly behind me to my right while I took in and was held in captivation and awe of the industrious activity of uniformed company employees and the considerable automated mechanical wonders and the sounds they made that was taking place all around me.

Interrupting my obvious amazement the director pointed to the far end of the factory saying over the automated din "Come Fraulein…we shall start at the beginning."

For the next hour during my guided tour the director would stop and indicate to me the various points of interest of the manufacturing process.

Starting as to where the castor beans entered the process…how they were crushed to make the very distinctive smelling castor oil then onto where and how the 'mash' was processed to make (what the director referred to as) medicinal ricin.

The one part of the large industrial process that I could follow and understand in this hive of personal and automated activity was the steady overhead metal conveyer parade from left to right of small clinking brown glass bottles.

Their progress (along with the distinctive sound they made) stopping at a station only long enough to be filled with a liquid…which I assumed to be either of a medicinal or therapeutic nature…once full…a cap was twisted on…a label applied and then the now full bottle with the others continued on its way.

Finally returning to where we had first started the tour the director turned in my direction and displaying the radiant pride a parent has for their exceptional child while reading my obvious expression, reacted to it by smiling then commenting "Impressive yes?" I admit that I was spellbound with what I had been shown.

But then the clues that had brought me to Germany and to where I was now I found were going in two separate directions.

I asked myself what undisclosed part of the factory was the ricin that was of the deadly poisonous nature being produced and where had the mustard gas (used in the war) that had brought me here in the first place been manufactured?

I waited and watched the grand pharmaceutical process continue for a few more minutes fully expecting to be invited to visit another part of the factory…when instead the only invitation I received was a final non-committal "do you have any questions Fraulein Morstan?"

To Herr Metzger's considerable surprise I returned "yes I do." It was something I had read in Dr. Briggs letter and seen labelled on barrels during the tour that I thought out of place that prompted me to ask "what does your company use acetone for?"

Displaying a similar reaction to the one I had seen at breakfast…but without the demonstration of cold military authority he calmly but unconvincingly replied (to me) "It is used merely as a solvent to clean machinery."

Chapter 25

Returning to the hotel after my morning appointment at Metzger Chemisch and while requesting my room key I was thankful to discover that in spite of my (no doubt widely anticipated) visit there were noun addressed envelopes awaiting my return.

Later during dinner that evening (the meal I ordered was rump steak or as we in the United Kingdom would know as roast beef served with various sides such as potato wedges and vegetables) while in the company of several other hotel dinner guests seated in the dining room I tried to make the two pieces of the puzzle I had acquired so far fit together.

Thinking to myself…while being aware of the low and quiet voices engaged in German dinner conversations carrying on at the other tables around me…that on the one hand I had located a manufacturer of delft porcelain that conceivably could have produced the blue bead which delivered the fatal poison and now a very potential source of the same poison that had ended John's life. But as of yet there was no way and no one to connect them.

Realizing that my investigation here was now at an end and noticing an alarming rise in social, political and military unrest that was starting to grip the population of the city of Dresden as well as the rest of Germany I thought it wise to leave this part of Europe and make my way by train back to the port of Calais…then home again to London.

In spite of experiencing some minor inconveniences with customs officials regarding my pass port while crossing national borders by train I expected to pick up where I had left my life when I returned.

However a week later when I resumed my volunteer duties there was an unexpected difference as to how I was welcomed back.

Patricia McLean one of the senior members of the Fawcett Society…also a member of Sinn Féin…Irish for "ourselves" or "we ourselves"(being an Irish republican political party), who had campaigned against the waging of the Boer War and the usage of conscription in the First World War was the first to draw unexpected and certainly unwanted interest regarding the nature of my lengthy absence.

She had caught me off guard when she stopped in front of me and unexpectedly asked "and Mary how was your trip to Johannesburg and Dresden?"

While gauging the reactions of the others around me who may have just overheard this and trying to construct a plausible answer that would deflect attention away from what was just said I looked at Patricia and I began to entertain a most improbable series of connections.

The rather austere and plainly dressed woman now standing before me…I knew to be a vocal supporter of the Social

Democratic Federation and the Independent Labour Party. In 1906 she joined the National Union of Women's Suffrage Societies and was imprisoned twice in Holloway gaol.

She became frustrated with the lack of progress the organization was making when she joined the more radical Women's Social and Political Union.

This last point set me thinking that with her past record of incarceration, unpopular views concerning conscription and present Irish political affiliation could she in some way have come to be associated with Willem Bastiaan van Steenwyk, Marius Bakeberg and Albrecht Metzger.

If true was this the possible motivation that had caused her to ask me (or been instructed to ask) such an out of place question.

# Chapter 26

Not having access to what John had referred to as a wealth of useful information...I would have to forge links or make connections with only the information I had acquired so far and had available to me.

Although I did not have enough 'straw' to make many bricks with yet...I felt that I had sufficient enough to begin.

The first common fact or event (as far as I understood) that connected all four had been their individual participation or involvement for whatever reasons, personal beliefs or financial gains to be made in the Great War

Second whether they had acted independently, without any knowledge of the others activities or if they had acted collectively (for whatever reasons) there had been one or a series of common denominators that had brought them in turn to my attention.

Because of what had taken place one evening at a ball in Johannesburg and the suspicion I had drawn from the event I was to find out shortly that I myself was one of the common denominators.

"The widow has been asking questions that are never to be answered...and she is making inquiries in places where she should not be. With that in mind what are we going to do about Mrs. Watson…or as she has taken to unconvincingly pass herself off as Miss Morstan?

"Certainly…I do not know who she thinks she is fooling with this charade? Anybody who has read the narratives of the late Dr. Watson (her husband) should know that the two surnames are linked."

"Can we simply do away with her? No…she is too well known and thought of…what with her established volunteer work…the famous deceased husband and well documented connection to and past collaboration with the consulting detective.

Removing her now would bring unwanted and unneeded attention. "Besides if she were to vanish…this would certainly give Mr. Holmes (where ever he is at the present time) great cause or reason to take up a trail that has been cold since 1917."

Chapter 27

Counterbalancing the somewhat cold and odd reception I had received upon returning to the society there was one person who was very pleased to see me again...my young friend Miss Elizabeth Humphrey.

I had first met her on a warm Saturday afternoon about a year ago at St. James's park. Regal St. James's Park (where John and I had picnicked together in the summer) it is surrounded by three Royal palaces.

Spanning 23 hectares (58 acres) it has a lake which is home to the park's famous pelicans. You can watch them being fed every day at 2.30p.m.so this is where and how we first met.

Of course I had seen Elizabeth at the park on previous Saturday afternoons and each time in my mind I had entertained the thought of being brave...overcoming my shyness...approaching her to say hello then introduce myself.

Except I was still coming to terms with Sherlock's absence...and missing my husband's company so I did not feel very confident or congenial when I should have.

However as I saw her on that particular Saturday...she seemed friendly and approachable so it was then I decided the time was right to let the world and the people in it back into my life.

Allaying what fears I might have I moved towards Elizabeth in what I hoped was a friendly manner…when I reached her I smiled and started with "Hello my name is Mary…Mary Morstan…and what is your name?"

---

She was at the time the newest member (at my invitation) of the Fawcett society…Elizabeth is the organist at St. George's Anglican Church…and she is employed as a stenographer by the law firm of Arnold and Porter (barristers and solicitors) which is located on Whitehall Street. She never married and lives at home with her parents Mr. Paul Humphrey and Mrs. Grace Humphrey.

---

A part of our conversation on our first afternoon together…after mutual introductions…that has always stayed with me was how she beamed then asked if I enjoyed reading mystery novels, and if I had a favourite author.

I answered (of course tempered with the life and the people I had known) "occasionally, but no I did not have a favourite author."

Elizabeth straight away came out and shared that she did and could easily lose herself in any of the works of Agatha Christie. I smiled to myself for a moment upon hearing the famous mystery writers name again as it brought back memories of a mystery writer I knew.

Deciding that I needed a friend who was well outside the sphere of everything Sherlock Holmes I did not bring up Winifred's name (or even my association to her) in the conversation but instead deftly changed the topic and started by telling Elizabeth about my early life as a governess in India.

Changing some of the details of the events that followed I told her as to how John and I had met. I went onto describe a quiet and somewhat uneventful life (certainly a fictional one for me) as the wife of a medical doctor until John's death in 1920.

My first day back with the Fawcett society ended on a positive note with Elizabeth inviting me to Koffmann's for a light supper then onto the Prince Charles cinema located at 7 Leicester Place to see a motion picture titled A Chapter in Her Life an American film based on the novel by Clara Louise Burnham.

After living on my own for so long with only my thoughts and fading memories for solitary companionship then alternately taking little notice of what I thought amounted to no more than the daily idle social gossip at the Fawcett society it was refreshing to listen to an interested and sociable voice while in the company of my young friend.

Despite the fact that there was some difference in our respective ages I found that Elizabeth and I shared many common interests and there was much we could talk about.

To any one seeing us together our conversation appeared to…and sounded as having the easy back and forth quality of old friends in terms of tone and character.

But like venturing out onto an only partially frozen over river in early winter I had to be careful where and how I tread so as to not break the ice and possibly fall through there by revealing my past with John and Sherlock.

---

From our first Saturday afternoon together, during the warm lazy days of summer and into the frost tinged days of fall Elizabeth and I kept amicable company.

Together we attended the Summer Exhibition. This is an open art exhibition held annually by the Royal Academy in Burlington House, Piccadilly in central London held during the summer months of June, July, and August.

The exhibition includes paintings, prints, drawings, sculpture, architectural designs and models, and is the largest and most popular open exhibition in the United Kingdom.

When the Royal Academy was founded in 1768 one of its key objectives was to establish an annual exhibition, open to all artists of merit, which could be visited by the public.

There was the Royal Horticultural Society Chelsea Flower Show, formally known as the *Great Spring Show*, is a garden show held for five days in May by the (RHS) in the grounds of the Royal Hospital Chelsea in Chelsea, London.

It is the most famous flower show in the United Kingdom, and perhaps in the world, attracting visitors from all continents.

We also attended the West End theatre. This is a popular term for mainstream professional theatre staged in the large theatres of what is known as the Theatre district located in and near the West End of London.

Along with New York City's Broadway and Hippodrome theatres, West End theatre is usually considered to represent the highest level of commercial theatre in the English-speaking world. Seeing a West End show is a common tourist activity in London.

Chapter 28

With the interval of time that had passed since departing from the port of Calais and returning home…revelations I had discovered, events I had experienced and the applicable information I had gathered while staying in Johannesburg and Dresden was losing its importance and had started to fade from my mind.

I found with time even my concerns about the mysterious circumstances surrounding John's death were also beginning to diminish.

With my overseas journeys now well behind me and days fully occupied with the Fawcett Society I felt I would eventually be leaving the exciting and liberating world I had known as a capable detective behind and return to the safe and anonymous role that of the widow of a medical doctor and as a volunteer.

But a member of Sinn Féin was determined that this was not to happen. Continuing the line of questioning she had started with on my return Patricia McLean persisted in wanting to know more about my (at the time unannounced) travels abroad.

As always carefully phrasing her query to sound merely as an innocent (or passing) comment she had recently questioned me on delft porcelain and castor beans.

While I could have easily dismissed her opening examination concerning my overseas destinations as mere coincidental curiosity…with the nature of her subsequent follow up questions each had started to link(in my mind) Patricia to Marius Bakeberg and Albrecht Metzger.

It was almost as if the two men, through Patricia were reaching across the distance to ask more about the true nature and purpose of my visits.

Adding to a rising feeling of discomfort with this unsolicited (and at times often unanticipated) attention I harboured a fear that other members of the society who had overheard these examinations may have become curious as to where my inquisitor was going with her line of questions.

With this they may well begin to ask similar questions of their own. It was at this point that I was beginning to treasure my secure and certain friendship with Elizabeth.

Chapter 29

"I see the widow has made a new friend...is this person someone we already have knowledge of or should we have knowledge of? No...she is of little importance to us but it is an odd co-incidence that this young lady (Elizabeth...I believe her first name is) has been seen regularly at St. James's park every Saturday since April.

One would get the impression that she had strategically placed herself there with the sole purpose of attracting the attention of Mrs. Watson."

---

"On another topic does the Fawcett Society member of Sinn Féin have any more information for us? No she does not and I have been informed the widow is getting agitated with being questioned by her.

Remarkably when Mrs. Watson chooses to answer...she still carries on as if she had travelled to the Union of South Africa and to Germany with the sole purpose of visiting with relatives and taking in the sites."

"What of the contacts (that we know of) she made while in Johannesburg and Dresden...was any information divulged that should not have been?

We have been assured no...but some of her comments and questions she made in both cities certainly did raise suspicion. We know that when she left the two locations she had little more than a general working knowledge of how delft porcelain and castor oil is manufactured."

"So we should not encounter any further problems with the former protégé of Mr. Sherlock Holmes then. Yes…from what has been learned by our member in the society Mrs. Watson is losing interest in her noble cause and appears to be quietly returning to what might be thought of as a civilian life.

There is however one small possible impediment concerning the widow's transition to retirement…What is that? It is Marius Bakebergin Johannesburg and the note he sent to the Monarch hotel. It was not addressed to Miss Morstan as it should have been but instead it was addressed to Mrs. Watson."

Chapter 30


Norway's Independence from Sweden(1905): After the Napoleonic Wars (1815), Norway was joined with Sweden, and ruled by the Swedish monarch Carl the III.

In 1905, the Personal Union between Sweden and Norway was peacefully dissolved, after Norwegian dissatisfaction with the union came to a boiling point. Instead of engaging in a war to maintain Norway, Sweden accommodated the countries desire for independence.

It was at this time a young family with the surname of Huber...being Norwegians of German decent moved from their small town of Farsund in the county of Vest-Gadder, Norway to East Finchley a borough of the city of London in the United Kingdom.

When the new arrivals had located and settled into suitable accommodations the father found work as a skilled optician. Within a short time the family became a part of the local resident German Émigré community.

Wishing to make a new start in their adopted country the father had suggested at dinner one evening and the family agreed that the best way to achieve this would be to anglicize their first and last names.

Their only child…a daughter they had named Liv…as any girl born in England was brought up in a loving and caring home.

She received a good education and excelled at her studies…was involved in all school as well as after school activities and was well-liked by her class mates…teachers and by the people in the local community.

However this would change when she (as a young adult) found herself taking an active interest in continental politics and the philosophies of the German Workers Party.

While on a visit home to Norway in 1922 the daughter found herself returning to a country much different from the one she had left as a child.

----

At the outbreak of World War I, Norway had bravely attempted to remain neutral but the country was wholly unprepared for any large military invasion.

In April 1914 German troops launched a major attack from the coast of Denmark. After crossing the North Sea in a short time nearly the whole country was occupied and under enemy control.

---

Torgeir Rendahl (July 18 1887) is a Norwegian politician. With the invasion of Norway in progress, he seized power in an Imperial German Army sponsored coup d'état. In 1914he proclaimed himself Minister-President and to the present day continues to govern in this role.

His government, known as the Rendahl regime, is dominated by ministers from Nasjonal Samling, the party he founded in 1903.

Despite the fact that many occupied countries were liberated by the allies during and towards the end of the war, Norway is still governed by the Rendahl regime with the backing of a foreign military occupying force.

# Chapter 31

It was a lead grey, overcast, still and silent late Sunday afternoon when I paused for a moment from the current Times crossword puzzle I had been pleasantly occupied with for most of the day. I put the paper down to look outside then become aware of the lingering foliage still crowning the trees lining both sides of Hill House Road.

Never really appreciating or being aware of it when leaving or entering the house and there for always taking its presence for granted I now observed through the window that the leaves had gradually started to transition from the familiar bright colours of autumn into the now dull and lifeless colours of early winter.

When each was fully transformed the tree released then let each individual drop away from its respective branch signifying that it no longer had any function and there for was of no further use.

I turned for a moment to contemplate John's journals still occupying the book shelves lining the study and realized that they too were now like the autumn leaves I had just seen and that they did not need to be where they were any more.

But unlike the changing seasonal event I had just watched unfold with each discarded leaf being let go then slowly spiral down one by one to the ground their final fate only to decompose with the cold rain I would lovingly collect and keep all of John's meticulously written notes in a safe, warm and dry place up in the attic.

With this final act of closure almost complete I would last gather up the final reminders of what had been an interesting and exciting life I had once known and place each in the box next to the now sleeping journals.

Before going back to what I had been engaged in I looked outside one last time as the bleak winter sun was beginning to set on the now barren trees of Hill House Road.

I watched as the first cold and fragile snowflakes of November one by one slowly and gently starting to spiral and descend from the sky.

The cover the snowflakes combined with a swirling winter wind together were starting to create was as fluffy white comforter that stilled all life under it.

In a similar manner all my memories of John, Sherlock, Albert Einstein, Winifred Jeffery and Harry Houdini were being covered with the passage of time...and were now being stilled and coming to an end.

---

Returning to my afternoon entertainment the next word in the cross word puzzle for me to solve was 7 across...it was a 13 letter word for an act that may under taken for financial gain, or to avenge a grievance…the word I found that fit the given number of boxes was 'assassination'.

## The Reporter (Gravesend)

The body of Doctor Michael Briggs 21years of age, long-time resident and general physician of Gravesend, Northwest Kent was discovered in the mid channel of the Thames and Medway Canal.

The crew of the local canal barge the Eliza returning to its home port were the first to happen upon the corpse. The immediate cause of death given at the time of discovery was by accidental drowning.

Dr. Briggs is the son of Dr George Briggs (retired from the faculty of medicine Imperial College London) and Mrs Catherine Briggs.

Born in London December 30, 1896, Doctor Michael Briggs completed his medical training in 1917 at Newcastle University. From 1918 (after returning from a medical internship in the Dominion of Canada) until 1923 Doctor Briggs had provided exceptional medical care in his surgery located at 65A Perry Street in Gravesend.

The doctor is survived by his parents and will be missed by his many patients attending at his surgery, by those in Gravesend and in the surrounding community who knew him.

Chapter 32

My first thought after reading this shocking story was to immediately contact Winifred, then quickly make plans to journey by train to Gravesend.

Once I had arrived and settled in she and I would work together and investigate the events leading to what I suspected was not an accidental death but the cold murder of the Doctor.

But I did not follow through with this plan because I realized that it most likely had been somehow discovered that Doctor Briggs had been forwarding to me relevant medial information (that was never meant to be shared) which had been of great assistance towards my uncovering the medical details of John's death.

Now experiencing some guilt due to our informal association I felt that the general physician's death had somehow been inexorably linked to the circumstances of my personal investigation.

With this conclusion I realized that the only knowledge Winifred might have of this matter would only have come from what she had read in the newspaper.

In the end I did not want to disturb her situation with any investigation as it might result in trouble or complications for her.

Feeling Sherlock's reassuring presence quietly standing behind me and watching me while I was seated at the desk in my study...I placed a blank piece of paper in front of me and with a fountain pen wrote down in succession four names...Willem Bastiaan van Steenwyk...Marius Bakeberg...Albrecht Metzger and Patricia Mclean.

Then I put the pen down and asked myself a series of rhetorical questions "which one of you had carried out this act...or are all of you somehow responsible for what happened in Gravesend?"

I followed with "what was so important...what wrong had to be righted...what message had to be sent that it cost the lives of two men who did not have to die" As if to respond to my last question I heard the echo of a familiar man's voice behind me reply "what indeed Watson?"

---

Then before my eyes appearing like the last long thin wisp of grey white smoke that rises into the late night time sky from the embers of an extinguished camp fire was the name Mata Hari.

---

Chapter 33


"With this Doctor Briggs now out of the way has the last of our 'leaks' been stopped up then?" "Yes"…"and was this early morning 'event' staged to look like some unfortunate accident?"…"certainly.

It will appear…for the moment any way that the young doctor somehow tripped while walking along the path next to the Thames and Medway…fell into the fast moving water…and because the current was too strong he was unable to swim to the canal bank and rescue himself…so he drowned."

"Well that should put an end to all of this then…it is regrettable we cannot replace a most important and valuable asset that has been lost to us…but I believe a strong enough and final message has now been delivered to all parties concerned that some events and the people involved in them are better left undisturbed."

If it was not for Elizabeth then the shock of the news concerning Dr. Briggs death would have taken a greater toll on me. However with the plans we had already made together for the Saturdays in November this helped me to relax and take my mind off as to how I might approach solving a second murder.

Before the beginning of my new friendship with her I had made several...at best half-hearted attempts (on my own) to leave my solitary home life for a short time to be among people again.

To motivate myself into doing this I had made the easy choice of going to the National Gallery...located at Trafalgar Square.

---

The National Gallery, houses one of the greatest collections of European paintings in the world. These pictures belong to the public and entrance to see them is free.

The National Gallery's permanent collection spans the period from about 1250 to 1900 and consists of Western European paintings.

Now I had an encouraging reason to attend and more importantly somebody to share the day with and comment about all the pictures the gallery had on display.

I have always been a great admirer of Queen Victoria who reigned from June 20 1837 until January 22 1901...this admiration however had not been shared by my late husband and was certainly not shared by Sherlock.

So it was a pleasant surprise when Elizabeth had suggested we visit the Victoria and Albert Museum on Cromwell Road, South Kensington. It is the world's greatest museum of art and design. The collection...including the personal possessions of her majesty the queen and Albert her prince consort is unrivalled in its diversity.

---

The Magic Hour is a unique magic show in the heart of London. Located near Hyde Park, and following sell out runs at the St Pancreas Renaissance Hotel and Hotel Russell, this highly recommended show takes place at the historic Grand Royale hotel. The show, performed in an evocative old drawing room, brings to life the illusions of the Victorian masters of magic

---

It was when Elizabeth had suggested going to this particular entertainment that I initially experienced a certain reluctance in accepting her invitation. For me to see any magic act would bring back reminders of all the events that had taken place while in New York City and of the last time I was with Sherlock at the Hippodrome Theatre.

But it was important for me to continue what had I thought had become a caring and supportive friendship that was certainly proving to be well outside the sphere of everything concerning the consulting detective so I happily agreed to accompany her.

---

The Victorian masters of magic whose illusions were brought to life during the first part of the afternoon performance were P. C. Sorcar then Robert-Houdin. After a short intermission were the illusions of Jean Eugène and David Devant.

It was during the intermission (while enjoying light refreshments, mingling and talking with the other guests) that as with our first conversation at St. James's park Elizabeth unexpectedly asked me in a similar tone and manner "Mary…when Mr. Houdini was performing here in London did you ever attend one of his matinee or evening shows?"

Chapter 34

In Article 231 of the Versailles treaty Germany was made to accept responsibility for the losses and damages caused by the war 'as a consequence of the...aggression of Germany and her allies.'

The article provided for Germany to compensate the Allied powers and to establish a 'Reparation Commission' in 1921 to consider German resources and capacity to pay, this gave the German government an opportunity to be heard (in principle) and to decide on the amount of reparations to pay.

In the interim the treaty required Germany to pay an equivalent of 20 billion gold marks ($5 billion) in gold, commodities, ships, securities or other forms.

The money would also be used to pay Allied occupation costs and buy food and raw materials for Germany, however as a rare concession to the defeated nation it would be allowed to continue to occupy Norway.

This most unpopular proposal had cautiously been put forward during the negotiations by the American President Woodrow Wilson and British Prime Minister David Lloyd George with very strong protests against the proposal coming from the French Prime Minister Georges Clemenceau.

Both the American President and the British Prime Minister were in favour of this plan (as they set out) because of having imposed such harsh terms. They did not want the defeated German nation to become belligerent with the intent of rebuilding its armed forces there for allowing it to restart hostilities now or in the future.

It was also reasoned by Wilson and Lloyd George that with this unusual compromise of allowing the defeated nation to keep occupied territory it would aid Germany in her ability to meet imposed financial obligations.

---

Bislett Stadion lies on the site of a 19th-century brick works, which was bought by the Municipality of Kristiania (Oslo) in 1898, and turned into a sports field in 1908.

The merchant, speed skater, gymnast and sports organizer Martinus Lørdahl was instrumental in facilitating the construction of the first bleachers, begun in 1917 and completed in 1922 along with the new club house.

This is the location the Norwegian government had chosen in 1919 to celebrate (with an evening torch lit political rally) each year the continuing cooperative and peaceful occupation of German troops and political governance of the country by the Nasjonal Samling party where Torgeir Rendahl would give his annual address to the nation.

It was during this immense (charged with an atmosphere of energy and excitement) gathering of the citizens of Oslo in 1922 that a naïve but enthusiastic young girl (named Liv) stood out and came to the attention of a German officer who (at the time) was dressed as a civilian.

He introduced himself as Erich Hoffman…after spending time with her during the rally…decided later that with what had been discussed (including her political beliefs) during their time together should come to the attention of III B-Chief Walter Nicolai.

Once easily persuaded to enter German service she was instructed about her duties by a Major Roepell. Her reports were to be sent to Düsseldorf under Roepell as well as to the Agent mission in the German embassy in London under Major Kalle, with her direct handler being the German officer she had met at the rally.

# Chapter 35

Fraulein Huber...please allow me to introduce myself to you...I am Major Roepell. To begin...your duties (when you return home) are to concentrate on a woman who resides in London, her name is Mary Watson. She is a widow who spends her days volunteering.

We believe Mrs. Watson may be in possession of certain important information concerning a woman named Mata Hari...she came to obtain it due to her association with a famous consulting detective.

In matters such as this we would appoint a junior officer to visit with her and gather it. However due to the sensitive nature of this material, Mrs. Watson's famous background, the people she presently has and had in her life and the 'troubling activities' she has recently been engaged in...this direct approach will not work.

We require a person she does not know but will be interested in meeting. Someone Mrs. Watson should have an instant affinity with...she should never harbour any reason to suspect this persons real intentions but will want to become friends with them...and that someone fraulein will be you.

First you will gain Mrs. Watson's confidence and trust then make her feel comfortable about opening up whenever you two are together.

Although you will be extensively briefed on her background (along with her association with a consulting detective) you are not to bring up, reveal or share any of this information while you are in her company.

From what we have learned and come to know of Mrs. Watson, with the exception of her volunteer work she leads a very quiet and solitary life.

Once you get to know her you will casually inquire from time to time as to what her interests are then encourage her to become involved in them again. Any activities that involve you and her taking place outside of her home will aid you with your task.

It will be when she feels that she is engaged in what she thinks is only light and safe conversation she will no doubt let her guard down and freely tell you what you need to know.

If there are any barriers that should arise to impede your developing relationship, bring them to my attention and I will deal with them. Finally it may be somewhat advantageous for you if Mrs. Watson were to be encouraged in suggesting your name for membership with the society she is already a member of.

Your first encounter with her should appear to be quite nonchalant...casual...almost co incidental. It has been well established that she is a frequent visitor to St. James's Park on Saturday afternoons so this is where your 'friendship' with her will commence.

You will be at this particular park on this particular day of each weekend where you will make yourself approachable…but remember you must let her first introduce herself to you.

You will meet with Captain Hoffmann on a once a week basis where you will pass along any information you have discovered or have learned from Mrs. Watson regarding the information we require.

Finally we have arranged transportation for you to return to your family and your place of employment…you will leave Oslo tomorrow morning to return to London.

# Chapter 36

After a time my friendship with Elizabeth started to take a curious turn. Granted I was puzzled at first about her comments concerning mystery writers then later her comments concerning escape artists…but with time I had put such things down to her age.

It was however as my young friend and I were leaving the Fawcett society each of us making our way home when as Patricia McLean was passing us both she gave me the unmistakable (I have more to ask you) look.

I tried not to react to what had been implied in that brief encounter…but with Elizabeth watching me she had read my expression and asked after in what I thought was a concerned tone of voice "do you know that person" and then after a short pause continued with "is there anything wrong Mary?"

Deciding (as we were walking together for a short distance) that I felt the need to express some of my concerns about past encounters with my inquisitor (in other words to someone I had come to trust) I revealed that Patricia had been asking me personal and uncomfortable details about my life.

To my considerable relief and yet at the same time surprise there were no follow up questions about this from

Elizabeth…her only comment was "I hope she will stop doing this to you soon."

It was only later when I started to discover my young friend's true identity and purpose that the unexplained reasons as to why she had not pursued the nature or direction of what had been asked by Patricia would be revealed.

My next clue towards her new behaviour came when she and I were having Sunday afternoon tea at Seven Park Place in the St James's Hotel.

As was our usual custom we sat together at a table where we could both watch the world (being the patrons of the tea room) pass by while we enjoyed the hotels fare and each other's company.

Always wanting to have my hand bag close I usually set it down in front of me and just to my right certain that it would not be disturbed.

This particular Sunday afternoon before I could stop its unexpected and unanticipated decent as the result of a waiter brushing past our table my handbag rapidly fell to the hard wood floor there by spilling out most of its contents.

As quickly as I could I bent over to replace scattered objects back where they belonged. To my surprise Elizabeth was suddenly in front of me on her knees eagerly helping in my task.

When she saw something from the scattered contents that caught her interest…being the cautionary note (still in its Monarch hotel envelope) that I had received in Johannesburg. Elizabeth (without asking permission) picked it up…looked at it and with a little more than just casual curiosity then inquired while now holding it up for me to see…"What is this Mary?"

Chapter 37


My last encounter with Patricia McLean before her
mysterious disappearance was when she thrust an article at
me that had been cut from the newspaper.

Her only biting comment while impatiently for me to take it
from her was "I believe you may find this of some interest
Mary…since having visited this city and met this person."

---

Mail & Guardian (Cape Town)

An employee of Loosdrechts Porselaina factory located in
the South African city of Johannesburg has been killed in
what is being regarded by police as an industrial accident.

The remains of a Marius Bakeberg were found next to a
damaged kiln that had been used in the manufacture of blue
delft porcelain. No one from the factory or the van
Steenwyk family could be contacted for comment
concerning either to the nature of the accident or of the
employee's position with the company.

Reading the newspaper clipping again I was taken back to
my time while in Johannesburg where I visited the
mentioned porcelain factory then to the Monarch hotel where
I had been staying at when receiving an anonymous (at the
time) note.

At that moment three very dissimilar facts suddenly connected. Because of the nature of the alleged industrial accident I realized I had now uncovered where the pellet that had been used to kill my husband was manufactured…and as the outcome of a business conversation and a misaddressed warning note there had been another murder.

Finally I felt sure I now knew the name of the person who was responsible for this shocking event and possibly for John's, Dr. Briggs and Marius Babenberg's deaths.

# Chapter 38

"What is this Mary?" Hoping that a one word answer would be sufficient to satisfy Elizabeth's immediate curiosity I (while putting the last of the strewn contents back in my hand bag) answered her "a note."

From her expression (as she was returning to her feet) to my quick answer I could tell she knew more about what she still had hold of than she wanted to admit to.

Suddenly any warmth of friendship in her voice dropped away when she coldly asked "an invitation…an appointment to be attended…a rendezvous perhaps?"

Finally finishing my task I also arose to my feet…reached over and quickly snapped the envelope away (to her considerable surprise) from Elizabeth's grasp…and replied back to her with equal coldness "a note."

---

As with my unpleasant association with Patricia Mclean ending there was no further contact with Elizabeth Humphrey.

While I was relieved that I would no longer be unexpectedly stopped and asked to give an account (by Patricia) of my overseas travels my former young friend's as of yet unknown circumstances of her disappearance had in a way convinced me  that I might finally be able to finally solve the reason, purpose and cause of John's death.

---

The tangled ball of yarn (that had been the people and events involved in John's death) began to untangle when I received an early evening telephone call from St. Bartholomew's hospital.

"Good evening Mrs. Watson…this is Dr. Lewis calling." Wondering to myself if after all this time the doctor had turned up any more information I courteously replied in turn "good evening Dr. Lewis."

In the course of our brief telephone conversation it was revealed that an anonymous letter (addressed to me) had been delivered to the hospital and left in the doctor's care with very specific instructions that it be given to only me.

---

Sitting down at my desk…like the parcel I had previously received from Dr. Briggs I looked at the envelope bearing only the first initial of my Christian name and that of my married last name with that I wondered what would be revealed when I opened it.

Searching until I found John's letter opener…cautiously I slit the cryptic envelope open to find it contained only two pieces of paper.

The first was a formal printed communique stating that an official delegation (headed by Willem Bastiaan van

Steenwyk) from the government of South African would be coming to London to call on the German embassy to establish trade agreements with German occupied Norway.

The second was hand written (somehow familiar to me) and far more informal in nature: *it would seem that Mr. van Steenwyk is in far more trouble than he realizes. Events he thought to have under control and kept out the light of day have gotten beyond his reach.*

*Three deaths and two disappearances have attracted unwelcomed and unwanted attention to certain individuals within the government of South African and the German government. This with your efforts in seeking answers concerning a personal death have made Mr.van Steenwyk an unwelcome individual everywhere.*

*You are close to solving your investigation. What remains will be available to you while the South African delegation is in London.*

*I have given you a telephone number where Mr. van Steenwyk may be reached. Arranging a meeting with him will be easy...as to whether he will co-operate with you or not will remain to be seen when you meet.*

---

"Prime minister there is a telephone call for you."

---

…"Say what you have to say Mrs. Watson…and express what you feel you must express concerning your allegations in reference to my perceived actions in this matter.

"I can give you (at most) between five and ten minutes of my time tomorrow afternoon before having to leave your company to attend an important meeting. We shall arrange to meet in the drawing room (which I believe will not be in use at that time) of the Grand Royale hotel at 1:50 p.m."

At 1:45 p.m. (the next day) I entered the hotel and quietly made my way to the appointed rendezvous. Crossing the foyer and entering the drawing room through the already opened doors instead of witnessing it occupied with an appreciative audience and a magician ready to amaze them with famous illusions there was only one person present…even with his back turned towards me I knew who it was.

When one of the floor boards creaked slightly under my step announcing my arrival he turned and addressed me.

"Please…come in and take a seat Mrs. Watson." Willem Bastiaan van Steenwyk invited me with some superficial graciousness while directing my attention towards one of the two dining room chairs located in the drawing room that were facing each other.

"I would prefer to stand" I heard myself reply in a surprisingly strong voice that quickly spurned his offer. "As you wish" he responded quietly. While sitting down in front of me on the chair to my right he took out his pocket watch to note the time of my entrance and as an unmistakable reminder to me that I would have precious little time to undertake my course of action.

Suddenly realizing that I was about to complete what I had originally set out to do (some time ago) at a gala ball held in Johannesburg...and because of this accomplishment I found that I was starting to tremble with a combination of genuine fear and yet oddly that of excitement with what was about to unfold.

Taking a deep breath as I stood before him I confidently began with what I had learned from my investigation as to what I thought were the reasons for John's unexpected and initially at the time unexplained death.

I described first (through the use of a combination of a toxic poison and ceramic pellet) the method of his death. Unfortunately this information had come with a price being the death of Dr. Briggs.

I went on to state that although I still did not know who had delivered the fatal blow...I implied that the man now sitting before me held some responsibility (if not all) for this action.

I stopped for a moment to gather my strength...then reflecting on my last time with my husband in hospital I continued. Although I did not know the exact reason why this man I was addressing had acted in the manner he had I felt that I was closing in as to why.

From the information I had learned from Mycroft Holmes, from my two overseas journeys, through reading John's journal, my association with Patricia Mclean and Elizabeth Humphrey I believe the motives for John's death were based solely on revenge against Sherlock for the loss of the spy Mata Hari.

Unfortunately due to Sherlock's "disappearance" after Mr. Houdini's show Willem Bastiaan van Steenwyk (and others) would refocus their attention and retaliation for wrongs or injuries received; then take vengeance on my husband for what they felt was a great loss.

Further this act would stand as a strong warning to Sherlock (for what he had done) and others not to look into or reveal the circumstances of or reasons for my husband's death.

Finally bringing my evidence against the former South African prime minister to a close I remained standing and silently waiting.

At that moment I felt as if a great weight should have been lifted from me but I was not certain it had because of the uncertainty as to whether he would either (unlikely) acknowledge or(possibly) refute my facts as they had been presented.

After (to my considerable surprise) paying close attention to (what I thought was) my well laid out evidence Willem Bastiaan van Steenwyk leaned forward slightly in his chair then gave me a familiar look any parent would give towards their failing child.

As if to reinforce this message he shook his head slightly from side to side indicating his disbelief. In a clear, yet obviously condescending tone of voice that left no doubt as to his underlying opinion of my evidence he began.

"Mrs. Watson...in all of this you have proven to be a very meddlesome and a tiring woman. You did not at any time have any right to seek out your answers in either Johannesburg or Dresden."

"I should inform you how ever what little if any information you gained in your 'investigation' was only in aid of discovering what you knew about the circumstances of your husband's death".

Here he paused to again to display his disappointment. "From my point of view with what has just related you have nothing of substance to go forward with other than what I see as at best as half-truths, and totally unsubstantiated facts."

He paused for a moment to let this opening and clearly defining statement take firm root in my mind then he continued...

"The events and details you have tried (might I say) unsuccessfully to connect to me today are nothing more than the labours of a fevered female mind.

Furthermore with what you have presented as so called incrementing evidence…is of such poor quality that it has only been arrived at by very unskilled and amateur detective methods. Sadly your fruitless pursuit has been guided by the disordered emotions of a grieving widow there for rendering it useless."

He paused again… then sat up and now took on the tone of voice and assured manner of a seasoned and experienced barrister confidently summing up his successful case before the jury in a court room.

"From what has been related to me…it has obviously not come from the sound mind of a professional, logical and trained detective such as Mr. Sherlock Holmes…who(it should be noted) if he were present would see that there is no basis or substance to any of your claims."

Finishing…as if now addressing and then requesting of the presiding judge to bring a forgone conviction of guilty against the accused our appointment came to an end.

"I would suggest Mrs. Watson that from now on you focus your attention solely to matters more suited to your gender and cease this pointless endeavour…and as well your very amateur attempts at being a detective."

"Too many people have come to an unfortunate end from either investigating or being involved in what should be seen as nothing more than an unexplained incident  happening on a London street."

Then without any pretence of civility Willem Bastiaan van Steenwyk silently rose from the chair he had been seated on…coldly turned his back to me and left the room.

---

Mr. van Steenwyk has finally become too great a liability to us…something must be done about this right away.

---

Chapter 39

Oxford Street (like any other busy street in the metropolitan city of London) at 3 p.m. on a week day is a noisy fast paced thoroughfare teeming with a blend of bustling pedestrians passing each other on either adjacent sidewalk and motor vehicles of all sizes, descriptions and functions travelling on the road between. Each vehicle motoring from their place departure to its place of arrival.

Additionally there is public transportation in the form of double-decker buses operated by the London General Omnibus Company for those who did not have personal use of a motor vehicle.

Further to the arterial flow on Oxford Street serving the commercial needs of the businesses located on the street there is a mix of small delivery vans and large heavy goods delivery lorries.

Since the transition from horse drawn vehicles in the 19th century to motor vehicles in the 20th century there has been a slow but steady rise in the number of vehicle and pedestrian accidents happening on city streets.

When the cause for the accident was investigated it was determined there was either a lack of attention on the part of the pedestrian or of the person operating the motor vehicle.

There have been a small number of fatal pedestrian road accidents where no clear cause could be determined or established.

However when the attending police constable was asked unofficially as to how this might have taken place it was often commented "you know…as improbable as this might seem it looked almost as if the person had been deliberately pushed from the sidewalk and into the oncoming vehicle traffic."

---

'Justice'(noun) as it has been defined in any authoritative dictionary is: the unbiased   administering of deserved punishment or reward.

Arriving at legal justice comes about by the due process of law where a claimant and a defendant each present their respective evidence before a magistrate or a judge of either guilt or subsequently innocence in the matter of committing a criminal act.

It is the final responsibility of the presiding magistrate or judge to evaluate the validity of the evidence given then determine as to where and how 'justice' will be served.

---

The right or wrong of the deeds committed by Willem Bastiaan van Steenwyk would never be formally presented in any court of law.

An impartial legal setting where he would have had the opportunity to face his accusers (me among many) without prejudice to plead his innocence or disavow any knowledge of claims that had been brought against him. Justice for him would be unexpected, swift and brutal.

---

From the time he had been caught off guard and brusquely pushed from the sidewalk by a seemingly anonymous pedestrian and onto the busy road he had little time to come to terms with the unsettling event that had just taken place.

As he was assessing any injuries to himself (from the fall) and getting to his feet while attracting as little attention as possible the former prime minister realized that he was going to be late for a meeting to attend and there for needed to return to the sidewalk.

At that same moment a final (and unspoken) sentence of justice was being handed down in the form of a speeding motor vehicle that would prevent him from ever reaching his intended destination.

The last thing Willem Bastiaan van Steenwyk ever heard or saw in his life was the sound of a petrol engine propelling the large rubber tyres of a fully loaded heavy goods lorry that was quickly and fatally bearing down on him.

# Epilogue

I decided that with the investigation of my husband's death now somewhat satisfactorily concluded and behind me…John could now finally rest in peace.

With these up until now troubling issues ended I felt it was time to bring some colour back into my life and also back to the house I lived in.

At that moment 'Brixton market' and the memory of an event that had taken place in 1920 involving a young female pick pocket came to mind.

But this time my reason for returning there would not be to prevent any criminal offence from taking place. Instead it was merely to purchase among other house hold items a large bouquet of flowers (which the market had been selling since 1870) to place in one of my favourite crystal vases when I returned home.

---

I had been leisurely walking about the busy morning market and taking in all its urban character for a time. First deciding what fresh vegetables I would need for meals the following week then after some other domestic purchases finally making my way to where the cut flower vendor stalls were located.

After being captivated by the vast floral rainbow of colours and their many wonderful fragrances that accompanied them that were presented before me I chose to take home a bouquet of pink and red roses.

Bending down for a moment first to take in their gentle perfume before purchasing what would be a pleasing addition to my home I heard from behind me what I thought to be a very familiar voice knowledgeably commenting on my forthcoming purchase.

"Roses are certainly an excellent choice to brighten any room. I believe the ones you are about to purchase are from the family Rosaceae…Subfamily Rosoideae…and genus Rosa if I am correct."

I stood up then turned in the direction of where the voice had originated from then hoped against hope that the expert observation I had just heard was that of a long lost friend.

When I realized it was…I smiled a shy smile and then to my considerable relief I heard myself say only a one word greeting "Sherlock!" he in return gave me one of his rare and not often shared with others warm smiles and returned with "Mary".

Mary Watson and The Departed Doctor notes.

To begin I would like to thank everyone who made this story possible...first to Carol Ann a friend and fellow writer who with her editing skills made a good story great. Then to the staff at the St. Paul branch of the Brantford Public Library...in Brantford Ontario Canada for providing a second home in which to write and conduct much needed research.

---

In Mary Watson and The Departed Doctor...Mary continues her narrative from Sherlock Holmes and The Escape Artist. In The Departed Doctor Mary Watson again takes up the task of detective and chronicler...She sets out to find the actual cause and reasons for her husband's - Dr. John Watson's untimely and unfortunate death.

---

Various characters and locations mentioned thorough out the story are drawn from other Sherlock Holmes case notes taken down by Doctor John H. Watson and later my his widow Mrs. Mary N. Watson

*While trying to make some sense of...and at the same time organize my collection of all things and events Holmes related I came across two unknown but remarkable documents dated from 1920.*

*Due to their size each had originally been put to use as a common book mark for Agatha Christies "The Mouse Trap and Other Stories" before they and the mentioned book had come into my possession.*

*Both documents unique significance had obviously been unknown or had been over looked by the previous reader of the book when employing them for this every day purpose.*

---

*The first...a personal note that Dr. Watson had written and given to his wife Mary just before his passing at St. Bartholomew's hospital asking her to take up the task (should she ever choose to) of chronicling future Sherlock Home's cases if the need should arise and if he (Holmes) ever decided to abandon his harsh and self-imposed exile.*

*The second...a copy of the obituary notice published in The Times which had also been circulated to all the other prominent London, United Kingdom and British Commonwealth daily newspapers containing the details of Sherlock Holmes close friend's untimely and most unfortunate departure from this life.*

When writing a fictional story writers are not bound by or to established facts or events as they unfold and can alter, change or rewrite them to suit the story.

In Mary Watson and The Departed Doctor the devastating events that happened in Germany during the Second World War were moved back to 1923 (after the First World War) to add  background and setting to Mary's arrival in Dresden Germany.

No good story is complete without some controversy. I achieved this by offering an alternate solution to the terms of the Versailles treaty.

I suggested as a way to prevent the eventual rise of Adolf Hitler and the National Socialist Party that Germany be allowed to keep at least some of the territory it had conquered and occupied.

As proposed (in the story) by the American President Wilson and British Prime minister Lloyd George instead of stripping Germany bare this would have allowed the nation to eventually repay its imposed debts and rebuild its self.

It would have emerged as a much different (and non-belligerent) country from the one that would eventually arise out the ashes of the Great War.

One final note…the mystery writer (Winfred Jefferies) that Mary Watson mentions throughout her narrative comes from the story "Sherlock Holmes and The Mystery Writer.

Fred Thursfield

## Also by Fred Thursfield

London 1895. A well known author, a theoretical invention made real, and the importance of a sometimes overlooked clue challenge Holmes and Watson to prevent the perfect crime.

## Also By Fred Thursfield

It is the start of the First World War. Sherlock Holmes is coaxed out of a short lived retirement to track down an exotic dancer to retrieve a secret accidentally given to her by a young patent clerk before it falls into the hands of a hostile government. As much a detective story as a brief history of the causes, reasons and the long term futility of a long forgotten war.

## Also by Fred Thursfield

Gravesend 1920. A famous mystery writer, while searching through the remains of a damaged church looking for story ideas, happens upon a document that was never meant to be found or read. Any knowledge of its contents could change the terms of the treaty that ended the First World War. There is also a change in the hand that writes and records the cases of Sherlock Holmes.

Do Spirits Return? Sherlock Holmes, Mary Watson, and Harry Houdini say 'No' and prove it.

# Also from MX Publishing

MX Publishing is the world's largest specialist Sherlock Holmes publisher, with over a hundred titles and fifty authors creating the latest in Sherlock Holmes fiction and non-fiction.

From traditional short stories and novels to travel guides and quiz books, MX Publishing cater for all Holmes fans.

The collection includes leading titles such as *Benedict Cumberbatch In Transition* and *The Norwood Author* which won the 2011 Howlett Award (Sherlock Holmes Book of the Year).

MX Publishing also has one of the largest communities of Holmes fans on Facebook with regular contributions from dozens of authors.

www.mxpublishing.com

# Also from MX Publishing

Our bestselling books are our short story collections;

'Lost Stories of Sherlock Holmes' , 'The Outstanding Mysteries of Sherlock Holmes', The Papers of Sherlock Holmes Volume 1 and 2, 'Untold Adventures of Sherlock Holmes' (and the sequel 'Studies in Legacy) and 'Sherlock Holmes in Pursuit', 'The Cotswold Werewolf and Other Stories of Sherlock Holmes' – and many more……

# Also from MX Publishing

"Phil Growick's, 'The Secret Journal of Dr Watson', is an adventure which takes place in the latter part of Holmes and Watson's lives. They are entrusted by HM Government (although not officially) and the King no less to undertake a rescue mission to save the Romanovs, Russia's Royal family from a grisly end at the hand of the Bolsheviks. There is a wealth of detail in the story but not so much as would detract us from the enjoyment of the story. Espionage, counter-espionage, the ace of spies himself, double-agents, double-crossers...all these flit across the pages in a realistic and exciting way. All the characters are extremely well-drawn and Mr Growick, most importantly, does not falter with a very good ear for Holmesian dialogue indeed. Highly recommended. A five-star effort."

**The Baker Street Society**

www.mxpublishing.com

www.ingramcontent.com/pod-product-compliance
Lightning Source LLC
Chambersburg PA
CBHW070044260626
47159CB00005B/2117